THE RIDDLE OF SAMSON

by Andrew Garve

"The story is an excellent one, the people are quite likable, and the writing is superior."
—*Springfield Republican*

"I think it is one of the most agreeably atmospheric, readable and sense-making jobs of its kind I have read in a long time."
—John W. Vandercook

"Mr. Garve is amusing company any time."
—*New York Herald Tribune Book Review*

Other titles by Andrew Garve available in
Perennial Library:

A Hero for Leanda
Murder Through the Looking Glass
No Tears for Hilda
The Ashes of Loda
The Cuckoo Line Affair
The Far Sands

The Riddle of Samson

By Andrew Garve

PERENNIAL LIBRARY
Harper & Row, Publishers
New York, Hagerstown, San Francisco, London

A hardcover edition of this book was originally published by Harper & Row, Publishers.

THE RIDDLE OF SAMSON. Copyright 1954 by Andrew Garve. All rights reserved. Printed in the United States of America. No part of this book may be used or reproduced in any manner without written permission except in the case of brief quotations embodied in critical articles and reviews. For information address Harper & Row, Publishers, Inc., 10 East 53d Street, New York, N.Y. 10022. Published simultaneously in Canada by Fitzhenry & Whiteside Limited, Toronto.

First PERENNIAL LIBRARY edition published 1978

ISBN: 0-06-080450-5

78 79 80 81 82 10 9 8 7 6 5 4 3 2 1

THE RIDDLE OF SAMSON

1

The day I crossed to Scilly the islanders had just learned that for the first time in their history they were going to have to pay income tax. The news had come straight out of the blue and they were visibly suffering from shock. On the boat from Penzance it was the sole topic of conversation among the home-going Scillonians. They were resentful, of course, and pretty caustic about the plight that "England" must be in if she had to scrape the barrel to that extent. Some of them aired their grievances to the tourists, taking the opportunity to explain the special circumstances that justified the islands' long immunity from mainland taxes, but most of them gathered in tight groups and debated among themselves. Not all of them were well informed about the exact nature of income tax and one anxious little man seemed to think that all his savings were going to be taken from him. I'd have offered a word of comfort but the moment didn't seem propitious—a hearty visitor who had just butted in with a crack about time being a great healer had had a distinctly cool reception. The fact was that on that April morning the friendly, easygoing Scillonians sounded capable of exposing a tax collector on Scilly Rock or even of seceding from the Commonwealth with a little more provocation.

In case you don't know the Isles of Scilly—the "Fortunate Isles," as the guidebooks like to call them—they're a cluster of five inhabited islands and nearly a hundred and fifty islets and rocks about three hours' steaming from Land's End. There was a time, thousands of years ago, when most of them were joined together in a single land mass, but the land sank and all the central part became a shallow, partially enclosed sea. To the south of this sea now lies St. Mary's, the biggest island of the group; to the northwest are Bryher and Tresco, to the northeast St. Martin's, and to the west the uninhabited Samson. On the outer fringes are the Eastern Rocks and the Western Rocks, with Agnes on its own across a deep channel to the southwest. The whole archipelago is on a miniature scale and to say that it occupies a sea area of about thirty square miles probably gives an exaggerated impression of its size. I suppose a modern airplane could fly from end to end of it in about a minute, and by motor boat you can get from any point in the group to any other point in little more than a quarter of an hour if the weather is good. The islands themselves are all very small—even St. Mary's is hardly more than two miles across and you can stroll right round any of the others—the "off islands," as they're called—very comfortably in a morning.

The total population of the group isn't much more than eighteen hundred and most of that is to be found on St. Mary's, the administrative center, which has a tiny "town" called Hugh Town, a harbor, hotels, shops, surfaced roads, a few motor cars and a little airport. In their time the Scillonians have carried on various occupations —fishing, piloting, wrecking, kelp burning, smuggling and market gardening—but now they seem to have settled for tourists and flower growing, particularly the latter. Having an average winter temperature about that of the French Riviera gives them a long start on everyone else when it comes to early marketing. So now almost every scrap of cultivable land on St. Mary's is laid out in bulb fields, which are sometimes no bigger than a few square yards and are nearly lost behind their tall windbreak hedges of pittosporum and veronica and escallonia. Incidentally, the flowers are picked in bud so the place is never quite the riot of daffodil and narcissus that most people imagine. The "off islands" are much wilder. They have their flower plots, too, in sheltered nooks around their tiny settlements, and Tresco of course has its "Abbey" and world-famous botanical garden, but all the northern part of Tresco and Bryher and St. Martin's is rugged moorland given over to bracken, gorse, and granite.

Unless you fly—and the planes from Land's End carry so few passengers at a time that it isn't always easy to get a seat—the only way to reach Scilly is by the R.M.S. *Scillonian,* which mostly does the trip on alternate days— out one day and back the next. She's not a bad little boat, but of course it's a very exposed stretch of sea and sometimes the crossing can be grim.

However, I was in luck that morning. The weather was superb as we chugged in among the islands, and for once there was hardly a breath of wind. The air was deliciously scented and in the sharp clear light the colors were unbelievably lovely. The sea was a vivid tropical blue as it nearly always is around Scilly—because of the absence of plankton in the water, the books say. Ahead, St. Mary's rose in gentle slopes of green and brown, with the mellow gray roofs of Hugh Town clustered on a narrow isthmus between scimitars of sand. Across the roadstead were more patches of color—the russet of twin-hilled Samson, the blazing gorse of Bryher, the pale gold beaches of Tresco against their background of dark trees. There was nothing ugly or jarring anywhere. The old London taxi on the quay and the two smart constables who constituted the whole police force of the islands seemed no more than amusing incongruities.

There was nothing hurried, either, as the *Scillonian* cautiously nosed her way into her berth. The men preparing to take her ropes and handle her cargo, the hotel porters with their hand trucks, the visitors and islanders who had strolled down to meet the ship, all moved with leisurely deliberation. Mainland urgencies had no place here. You could almost see the passengers relaxing as they stepped ashore and wandered off without formality to find their hotels in the miniature town.

The first thing I did on landing was to look around for my gear. I'd written to Barney Randall—a boatman who ran one of the inter-island launch services and whom I'd come to know rather well on previous visits—asking him if he'd mind ordering locally some of the heavy things that I couldn't easily bring down with me. And here they all were, stacked on the quay under a tarpaulin—a galvanized wheelbarrow, half a dozen big planks, a pick and shovel, two four-gallon cans for fresh water and another can for paraffin, and quite a lot of other stuff besides. I added the army entrenching tool that I'd carted all the way from London because it was particularly good in sand, and let the porter take the tent and sleeping bag and the big suitcase to the Ocean Hotel, where I was booked for one night.

As I followed him along the narrow main street, past the chemist's shop and the chalked boards announcing which of the islands the motor boats were visiting that day and the window with the shapely bottles of Cornish mead "made by the Druids 400 years ago," I was sharply reminded again that this was Scilly's "Black Day." Although it was lunchtime, quite a few people were standing in the road talking to those who had just come off the boat with news from the grasping mainland. A young workman in dungarees and a cloth cap who had evidently been drowning his sorrows was reeling from group to group calling out in a loud voice, "This tax 'ave 'it me 'orrible!" Outside the Town Hall, a placard said "Protest Meeting 8 P.M." Even in the hotel there was no getting away from the subject, for the unheralded arrival of four newspapermen from London by special plane that morning had complicated the room arrangements and it took a little time to get me fixed up.

Most of the guests were taking advantage of the fine weather to spend the whole day on one or other of the "off islands," so I lunched almost alone. I had a big program for the afternoon, laying in stores, and directly the shops reopened I borrowed the hotel's hand truck and went off with the list I'd drawn up. Apart from the considerable amount of food that George and I would need there were all the cooking utensils to get, as well as the hundred-and-one minor articles you've got to keep by you when you're camping on a desert island. I had to make several journeys, and when all the stuff was stacked up in

5

the Ocean's annex it looked as though a major expedition were about to set off into the unknown. I dispatched a card to George telling him that everything was under control and then went for a stroll round the little western peninsula of the island called the Garrison, which is famous for the fact that in the Civil War the King's men were still holding out there against Parliament years after everyone else had stopped fighting. Apart from its historical associations, I always think that it offers about the finest short walk in Scilly.

By the time I got back to the Ocean the launches had returned with their loads of holiday makers and the spacious bar was beginning to fill up. I'd arranged to meet Barney there but he hadn't arrived yet so I ordered a half of bitter and turned to see what sort of company the evening had brought. It was a pretty mixed crowd. There was the usual bunch of high-spirited girls with wind-polished cheeks and peeling noses, flirting with the boatmen and clamoring to be taken round the Bishop Lighthouse. There were two eager young people arguing whether a bit of stone they'd picked up on Bryher that day was moss agate or not, and there was a youngish man in well-cut tweeds discussing bird watching with a white-haired old boy in a blazer. There was a party of four women together, probably schoolmistresses, with stout shoes and bramble-scratched legs, and two couples sibilant in corners who were stamped all over as honeymooners. And of course there were the locals—the flower farmers and shopkeepers and businessmen, still harping on the iniquities of the Chancellor of the Exchequer.

Presently there was a new and noisy influx. Five men, who appeared to be carrying on a running argument, swept in like a minor avalanche, preceded by a most striking-looking girl. She was dark, and tall for a woman, and though her expression was too hard and aloof for my taste she had a highly individual kind of good looks. It was her clothes that caught everyone's eye, though. She was wearing a pleated tartan skirt in dark greens and a black turtle-neck sweater and a cream leather jacket with a lot of heavy black stitching on it and nylon net stockings and beautiful shoes in hand-sewn natural leather. The general effect was extremely elegant but a bit spectacular for Scilly—it was the sort of rig-out you see advertised as smart holiday wear in the glossier fashion magazines. She seemed a little detached from the rest of her party and after she had accepted a glass of sherry from one of the men she turned away rather coldly and gazed around the room in a haughty, self-possessed way, obviously sizing everybody up. She got some pretty fierce stares in return and the collective antagonism of the windswept girls with their bare legs and ankle socks and tankards was palpable.

At first I couldn't place the new arrivals at all. They were certainly not residents and although they were lively enough they lacked the invincible cheerfulness of holiday makers. It wasn't until I heard one of the men say something about an "interview" that I realized they must be the Press. Four of them were quite young fellows, neatly dressed and "towny" and rather nondescript. The fifth, who was wearing a sports jacket and flannels and a checked wool shirt, was considerably older and a lot more impressive. He was a big man, with a rich brown beard and mustache, a deep resonant voice, and the heaviest pair of horn-rimmed glasses I'd ever seen. It was he who'd been doing most of the talking as they came in, and as soon as they'd got their drinks he leaned back against the bar, very much at his ease, and continued to hold forth as though he were conducting a seminar. He gestured freely as he talked, waving in one hand an enormous empty pipe and in the other a bulging tobacco pouch. He was aggressively uninhibited and was talking about the Scillies and the Scillonians as though they were something under a microscope rather than a living—and potentially resentful—reality all around him.

"The Fortunate Isles?" he said rhetorically, ramming tobacco into his pipe and spilling about half an ounce on the floor. "I'll say they're fortunate. Pampered's the word. Just look at the money the Duchy's spent on them! Look at the visitors who come pouring in all the year round! Look at the flower industry! You're not telling me the farmers don't make fortunes out of a hundred million flowers a year?"

"Eighty million, Ronnie," said a stocky little man in a tone of mild reproof.

"Well, eighty million, if you like," Ronnie said. "Whatever the figure, they're still rolling. Look at the dough that chap left in his will the other day—twenty-two thousand pounds! No wonder they can spend their holidays in Cannes and Bermuda! I wouldn't mind betting a lot of them are making a cool five thousand a year. They've nothing to squeal about—they ought to have been taxed long ago." He took a gulp of what appeared to be neat whisky and began to light his pipe, blowing out a huge cloud of smoke and a shower of sparks. Between puffs he kept glancing across at the girl as though seeking her approval of his harangue.

The stocky man said: "That's all very well, but this tax is going to hit everybody, not just the wealthy farmers. It's bound to mean higher freights, and you can't get away from the fact that prices here are already far above those on the mainland. Elevenpence for a loaf of bread is no joke, after all, and . . ."

"I agree," Ronnie interrupted, "but *why* are prices so

high? Because the chaps who run the boats are piling up whacking profits—that's why. They're simply soaking the rest of the islanders."

A pasty youth with long hair and a supercilious expression said: "Easy, old boy, we're not alone."

"Personally," said the stocky man, dropping his voice, "I reckon they earn every penny they get. It must be damned hard work keeping a service going in all weathers —and pretty hazardous, too, at times."

"Hazardous? My dear chap, there's nothing difficult about these waters. All you've got to do is study the rocks at low tide and after that it's child's play."

"Damned precocious child!" said the stocky man.

Ronnie ignored that. "Now where I learned my sailing, in the Thames Estuary, it really is tricky—mudbanks everywhere and not much shelter. Here you've only got to watch the bottom and keep inside the islands and you can't go wrong."

"Then how did you manage to crack that plank in *Truant?*" asked the supercilious youth.

"Hell," said Ronnie, "you can't avoid rocks when a boat's almost out of control. With the mizzen gone and only a jury rudder I was darned lucky to reach an anchorage at all." He drained his glass and looked inquiringly around. "What about some more drinks?"

The girl shook her head. The others had beer and Ronnie stuck to whisky. He produced a bundle of loose notes from a side pocket and flung one of them carelessly on the counter.

"Anyway," persisted the stocky man, "I still think you're wrong about the boatmen. There's a lot of competition, don't forget—and look at the capital they've got tied up. Those big launches cost anything up to a couple of thousand."

9

"The trouble with you, Bill," said Ronnie, "is that you don't understand economics and you believe what people tell you. That flower farmer we talked to this morning, for instance—why, the figures he gave us were as phony as he was. When I saw you solemnly taking them all down I nearly died. . . ." Suddenly Ronnie's features seemed to crumple and change, and he began to talk in an affected drawl that was obviously intended to be an imitation of someone they'd all met. It must have been a good imitation, too, for there was a gale of laughter, in which the supercilious youth joined. Even the girl gave a fleeting smile.

I lost track of the reporters after that. As I turned to have my own glass refilled I saw that a man standing beside me had a map spread out on the counter—and a map, even a familiar one, is something I always find it hard to resist. He was an odd-looking character of about my own age—very spare and angular, with bony wrists and knobbly sunburned knees lapped by a pair of gray flannel shorts that looked as though they'd been cut down from "longs." At his feet there was a rucksack of crippling size. He seemed a friendly soul and we soon fell into a typical Scillies conversation about the islands and their comparative attractions. This, I gathered, was his first visit, and he was full of enthusiasm and determined not to miss anything. He'd been in the place for only three days but he'd already explored Tresco, Bryher and St. Martin's, besides taking in the eight-mile coastline of St. Mary's in a morning. He liked walking, he told me, not only for the interest but for the exercise.

"Don't you find the islands a bit cramping?" I asked him.

"Well," he said with a gentle smile, "I do sometimes go round them twice. As a matter of fact I was just wondering if I could give myself an extra mile or two by walking across from Tresco to Samson? It looked today as though it might be possible."

"Oh, yes," I said, "that's perfectly feasible if the tides are right."

"The boatman was saying this morning that they're going to be exceptionally low for the next few days."

"In that case you should have no difficulty at all. Samson Flats run out almost to Tresco and I've often seen the channel practically dry in between."

He looked pleased. "Then I think I'll have a shot at it tomorrow."

"If you want to do something really strenuous," I said, "why not try walking from here to Tresco and then on to Samson?"

He looked through the window at the blue expanse of sea. "From here to Tresco! You don't mean that, surely? The roadstead can't be as shallow as that."

"No, but further along there's a sand bar—Crow Bar, they call it.* It runs from Bar Point on St. Mary's across to Tobaccoman's Point on Tresco, and the distance isn't more than a mile." I indicated the route on his map. "Some people say it's an old Roman causeway, but there's no evidence for that. I'm inclined to think it's a huge natural sand dune that's been slowly eroded."

"And it actually uncovers at low water?"

"I don't know that it's ever quite dry, but there wouldn't be more than a foot or two at low water springs and that would only be for a short distance. People certainly have crossed."

"It would need pretty careful timing, I should think."

I agreed. "It certainly wouldn't do to get caught. The spring tides run very strongly over the bar."

* See sketch map.

11

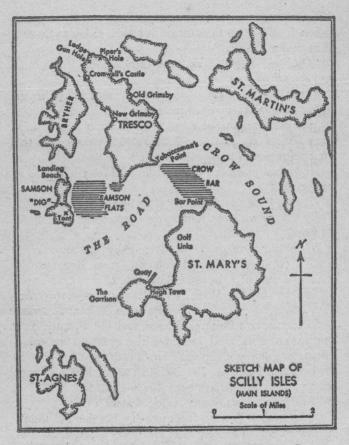

SKETCH MAP OF
SCILLY ISLES
(MAIN ISLANDS)
Scale of Miles

He pondered. "Well, I think I'll try the Tresco-Samson bit first and see how I get on."

We talked a little longer, and then he picked up his rucksack and went off to change. He'd only just left when Barney came in and joined me at the bar.

Barney's about forty. He's small and inclined to be

plump, and with his clear-cut features and dark smooth hair and sardonic eyes he always makes me think of the pictures of Napoleon Bonaparte. It takes quite a while to get to know him, but it's time well spent. He has a very dry wit, and the ways of mainland visitors, quietly observed over more than twenty years, give him plenty of scope to exercise it. Yet he's kindly and courteous and unfailingly obliging to those who put themselves in his care —I never knew a man with a greater sense of professional responsibility. His interests tend to be parochial, of course —but what a parish! He can tell you where to look for baby seals and where the puffins are thickest and which beaches have the cowrie shells and how much fish a shag eats in a day; he's wise about the moods of the sea and the quick-changing weather; he prides himself on his craftsman's skill and on knowing every rock and shoal and current around the islands. And that, in these flower-growing days, is an increasingly rare thing.

We shook hands and I called for another pint. "Well," I said, "leaving income tax out, how's things?"

He pushed his peaked cap back from his forehead. "Can't grumble," he said, and took a long pull. "We've got another boat since you were here last."

I looked at his blue jersey and saw that the name *Seagull* had been embroidered below *Tern*.

"Nice work. What's she like?"

"Thirty-foot launch. Old—but sound."

"Fine. And how's Jim—still breaking the girls' hearts?" Jim was his nephew and right-hand man in the business.

Barney gave a reminiscent chuckle. "He had three of them cleaning the brass last week."

"There's safety in numbers, anyway."

"That's what the missus says. I expect he'll settle down

in the end. He's been doing a job on his own account this winter, you know."

"Oh?"

"Yes, he's been repairing a boat for a private owner." Barney jerked his pipe stem in the direction of the reporters. "Big chap with the beard. I wasn't too keen on the idea at first, because of all our own fitting out, but Jim was eager to make a bit extra so I had to let him have a go. And I must say he's done a darned good job on her. She was in a proper mess when she got here."

"What happened?"

"She was caught out in an easterly gale—last September, it was—and got blown all the way from the Lizard. Trouble was he was sailing her single-handed, and she's a bit big for that." Barney took another drink. "I suppose you saw your stuff on the quay?"

"Yes, I did. Thanks very much—I'm most grateful."

"No bother at all. When's Mr. Curtis coming down?"

"Tuesday week, he hopes. It's a pity he couldn't make it earlier, but at least I'll have most of the heavy work done by the time he gets here."

"When would you like me to take you across?"

"As soon as you can."

Barney considered for a moment. "I could take you to-morrow morning early—say seven-thirty. The tide'll be right for unloading then."

"Good. I'll see the porter about getting the rest of the stuff to the quay. There's rather a lot of it, I'm afraid."

"We'll manage. Will you want a punt while you're there, by the way?"

I'd been wondering about that. If I had my own rowing boat I should be more independent, of course, but I didn't expect to be doing a lot of moving about once I was installed and the launch service was pretty adequate.

"I don't think I'll bother," I said. "You must be doing fairly frequent trips now you've got *Seagull* as well."

"Yes, we're doing the same as the other chaps now. Leave here at 10:15 in the mornings, call at Samson, Tresco and Bryher, and back at 12:15 with anyone who wants to have lunch on St. Mary's. Then out again at 2:15 and back about five, same itinerary. And of course some special trips as well according to how the weather is. We've taken on a couple of lads to help."

"Big business!" I said.

"It's coming on." Barney glanced at the clock on the wall. "I'll have to be pushing along or the missus'll be complaining. Can I buy you a drink before I go?"

"Another time, Barney—I've had all I want for now."

"Cheeroh, then—see you on the quay." He drank up and went out quickly, nodding to a bunch of his customers on the way. The Randalls never missed a chance of being pleasant. It was good policy, but it also came naturally to them.

There was another burst of laughter behind me and I swiveled round to see how the newspapermen were getting on. Ronnie's face was deeply flushed and he was still drinking whisky and still hogging the conversation. The girl seemed more detached from the rest of them than ever. She was standing close beside me, toying with an almost empty glass. Our eyes met, and after a moment she said in a rather bored voice: "Have you just arrived?"

I nodded. "This morning, on the *Scillonian.*"

"Do you know the islands at all?"

"Fairly well. This is my fifth visit."

"Heavens! You must be an addict."

"People either love them or hate them, I find. Which do you?"

"Well, as I've hardly been beyond the end of the quay

15

I'm not really in a position to say. Their policemen are wonderful, of course!"

"Aren't they! Both of them!"

"What do they do besides watching the *Scillonian* come in?"

"Well, they watch her go out. . . ."

She laughed, and at the sound Ronnie suddenly stopped talking and gave me a penetrating stare. The master of ceremonies evidently objected to a diversion.

I said: "What paper are you on?"

She looked surprised for a moment. Then she said: "Oh, I'm not a reporter. I'm only married to one."

I hadn't noticed her ring. Now I did, and the huge solitaire diamond she was wearing above it. From Ronnie's sharply proprietorial look, I concluded that it was to him she was married.

"My husband's on the *Record*," she said. "We really came down here to collect a boat and take a few days' holiday. Then this wretched story broke and of course the office rang and asked him to cover it and he's been hard at it ever since. I'm an income-tax widow."

"Too bad!"

"It's perfectly maddening. Like going to heaven and hearing nothing but talk about the price of harps!" Her tone was disgusted.

Now that I came to study her more closely it was obvious that she wasn't a reporter. No girl who'd been racketing around on a story all day could have stayed as soignée as that. I also had to revise my ideas in another respect—despite her rather cold expression I found her tantalizingly attractive. Her forehead was high and smooth, and her green eyes were set slightly on the slant, which increased the general effect of hauteur. She had the sort of face you could go on looking at without tiring because everything wasn't in the shop window. And her hair was lovely—thick and wavy and almost black.

There was a little pause, and then she said, "Are you here on holiday or on business?"

"A sort of holiday," I told her. "As a matter of fact I'm going out to Samson to do a bit of digging."

"Digging?"

"Yes, digging for old ruins."

"You mean you're an archaeologist?"

"Only as a hobby. I lecture on Modern History for a living."

Her eyes had taken on a sparkle of interest. "Where?" she asked.

"London University."

She looked me up and down and it took her quite a while. "I should never have thought you were a don," she said.

"They come all sizes, you know."

"I'd call you outsize," she said dryly. "What ruins are you going to dig for—anything special?"

"Oh, yes. About thirteen hundred years ago some Celtic saints came to Scilly and established monastic cells on several of the islands. We're hoping to discover the site of the chapel that St. Samson built for himself. A friend of mine is joining me later."

"Then is all that stuff in the annex yours?"

"The pots and pans? Yes, we'll be camping out for a week or two."

"Samson's the island that was evacuated, isn't it?"

"That's the one."

"It sounds quite amusing," she said. "I wish you luck."

At that point the dinner gong sounded. People began to drift out of the bar and Ronnie called, "If you're going to change, darling, you'd better hurry." He gave me a

17

frosty look, which I thought preposterous, and the girl, without another glance at me, walked disdainfully out of the room ahead of him.

Ronnie was still voluble at dinner. He'd put away a prodigious quantity of whisky but he appeared steady enough when he went off with the other reporters just before eight to attend the Protest Meeting. I strolled along too, out of curiosity, but it proved to be for "Residents Only" and anyhow the small hall was so packed that there wasn't even standing room. Back at the hotel the atmosphere was oppressive—someone had turned the electric fire on in the lounge and there were at least three honeymoon couples sitting around waiting for nine o'clock to strike so that they could decently go to bed. I decided to set them an example and call it a day.

2

The Randalls had been at the quay for some time when I turned up just before half past seven next morning. Barney was out at *Tern's* moorings, preparing to bring her in to the stone steps in the inner harbor, and Jim was busy moving my gear to the same spot, ready for loading. He broke off when he saw me, and we greeted each other cordially.

I'd always liked Jim Randall. When I'd first met him he'd been an eager youngster of twelve, tow-haired, merry-eyed and impulsive, and utterly devoted to Barney. That wasn't surprising, for Barney had not only shouldered responsibility for him after the death of the elder Randall brother—he'd personally taught him to swim and fish and sail and calk decks and tinker with engines and in fact do all the things that an active boy most delights in. Boats, and the skills of the sea, had been Jim's life, and for years he'd sat contentedly at Barney's feet. Now that he was a husky giant of twenty he was growing a bit restive. On the surface he appeared an effervescent, happy-go-lucky young hedonist, enjoying his work and his flirtations and his blue-water existence, but from casual remarks he'd let drop the previous summer I knew he was chafing. Barney's idea was that in the fullness of time Jim would qualify to be an equal partner in the business but that meanwhile there could be no question of divided authority. Jim had ambitions beyond the confines of Scilly, and the restraints imposed by Barney were beginning to irk him. It wasn't that his respect and affection for his uncle had diminished, but he had his full share of the independent Randall spirit and I felt certain that sooner or later he'd strike out on his own.

I helped him to move the rest of the stuff and then we stood chatting on the quay, waiting for *Tern*. Our talk was mostly about boats—not that I'm anything but a tyro myself but you can't spend many holidays in Scilly without picking up a smattering of knowledge. Tom pointed out, with evident pride, the thirty-foot ketch that he'd repaired during the winter, and I admired the low fast lines of *Seagull* and also a new white punt attached to *Tern* which he said was about the handiest to row that he'd ever come across. Presently Barney drew alongside and we quickly loaded up. A few minutes later we were sliding past the pale green hull of the *Scillonian*, which was getting up steam ready for her own departure at nine. There had been a change in the weather overnight—the wind had gone round to the east and freshened and at that early hour I was glad of my warm sweater. But the outlook was promising. The sky was cloudless and there was a thin haze over the islands which Barney assured me meant a dry spell.

It was an exhilarating crossing, for the wind had knocked up some white horses in the roadstead and a good deal of spray was coming aboard. We spread a tarpaulin over the gear and then I stood balancing in the bows, picking out half-remembered sea marks, while Barney and Tom discussed which boat should do the regular run that morning and whether Agnes or the Eastern Rocks would be the better proposition for the other one. By the time they'd reached a decision and sorted out their respective tasks the powerful forty-foot launch had eaten up the two miles of sea and we were closing in on Samson. The island has no harbor or pier and the usual landing place is a sandy beach at the northern end opposite Bryher, but today we were cutting across the well-covered flats and making for a point about halfway up the eastern shore in order to save me hours of porterage. The tide was still pretty high, but ebbing, so we anchored some distance out and Jim proceeded to ferry the gear ashore in the punt. He dropped me with the first load, on a narrow strip of beach under a low sandstone cliff, and went back for two more loads. There was enough of a sea to make it awkward going for him but everything passed off without a hitch and in next to no time Barney was hauling up the anchor and they were waving me a cheery farewell.

When they'd gone I scrambled up the six-foot cliff and gazed around with satisfaction at what, for an hour or two at least, would be my private domain. Samson is not, of course, the loveliest island in the Scillies and some people find it melancholy, but it has a lot of atmosphere and it's always been one of my favorites. It's rather less than a mile long from north to south and it's shaped like an hourglass. The waist, a mere hundred yards across, is sandy and low-lying. The bulges to north and south rise quite steeply, each to a hill a little over a hundred feet high capped by impressive granite boulders. Except for the waist, practically the whole island is a tangle of bracken and brambles and heather and coarse turf, but there are several paths which the visitors have kept open. On South Hill there are some stone walls and the remains of seven or eight cottages which have been gradually falling to bits since the island was finally evacuated in the 1850's. There are a few domestic middens, some of them telling a story that goes back three thousand years or more, and up on the cairns there are many interesting megalithic barrows and burial chambers. And that's about all there is of Samson.

Barney had set me down at the waistline, at a spot conveniently close to where George and I would be digging, and all I had to do with the heavy gear was to sling it up on the grass and make a dump. It wasn't so easy to decide where to pitch the tent. The waist was totally unprotected —apart from two small boulders and a few thistles and patches of yellow moss it was as bare as a well-worn football field, which in appearance it rather resembled. If I camped there and a gale got up from the east or the west I'd be blown clean into the sea. The trouble was that there wasn't a great deal of flat ground anywhere else. On the principle that those who had actually lived on the island must have discovered the best spots, I set off to reconnoiter the slopes of South Hill. There was a path of sorts leading to a wall across the southern end of the waist, and a crumbling V-shaped stile, which I crossed. Beyond, there were several hollows that offered fair shelter but the ground was covered with ferocious brambles and I didn't fancy the job of clearing them if it could be avoided. I climbed higher, picking my way through the crackling undergrowth. I passed a tumbled ruin with a stunted tamarisk in the garden—the only tree on the island apart from an elder or two—and presently I reached another cottage, in slightly better shape. It was open to the sky, but it had four solid granite walls, with holes where the door and windows had been. All the stonework was covered with a pale gray-green lichen and ferns grew bright in the crannies. The whole place measured about twenty feet by ten. There were some big stones inside at the foot of the walls, but in the center there was a clear space covered with short turf. It looked clean and inviting, and I decided there and then that this was the site for our camp. It would be a snug spot in any weather.

I returned to the waist at a leisurely pace and fetched the tent. It was a lightweight affair, a bivouac tent for two, with a fly sheet. It went up beautifully once I had managed to drive the pegs into the hard ground, and it looked very neat and secure. I slashed off the heads of a few stinging nettles which were growing rather too near the entrance for comfort and then went back down the hill for another load. There was a tremendous amount to carry—the suitcase and the sleeping equipment, the water and the paraffin, the oil stove and the crockery, and all the food. I still hadn't finished when, a little after half past ten, I turned my binoculars on a white boat slipping past the southern end of Tresco and saw that it was *Tern* on her routine outward run. As I watched she made a wide sweep to the west and began slowly creeping along the edge of Samson flats toward the landing beach. It looked as though I should soon have company.

The sun was beginning to get hot now and before long I was sweating freely in spite of the breeze. On the next climb to the tent I carried a bottle of beer with me and sat down on a soft cushion of sea thrift to cool off. I felt glad that I had no urgent schedule to get through for it was most pleasant out there on the hillside. The appearance of the sea and the islands had changed enormously since my arrival that morning—the water in the roadstead was now a delicate aquamarine, with deep purple shadows where the rocks and weed approached the surface. Above me, a dozen black-backed gulls, heads to wind, floated effortlessly on an upcurrent of air. At my feet, peeping through the old dry bracken, were vivid patches of bluebell and celandine and violet. As always, the scent was exquisite. I wondered what George was doing at that moment, and what he would give to exchange his slide rule and logarithm tables for the freedom of Samson.

By the time I felt ready to make a move the tide was right out and great areas of pale sand and mottled gravel were exposed. Samson flats were dry for half a mile offshore and I could clearly see the remnants of a man-made wall below high-water mark which offer one of the clearest proofs that the land of Scilly has sunk. In the distance, only a narrow strip of water separated Samson from Tresco. I had just got to my feet when, away on the Tresco side, I spotted a man picking his way over the weed-covered rocks toward the channel. At first I didn't recognize him, even through the glasses, but as he came closer I saw that it was the fellow with the knobbly knees and the cut-down shorts. He looked an even stranger figure today, for he'd slung his boots round his neck and his long lean legs were bare. Evidently he was carrying out the program he'd outlined to me the previous evening. I watched him approach the channel and try it for depth, but it seemed that he was a bit premature or else he'd picked the wrong spot. He went in until the water was lapping round his shorts, stood for a while hesitating, and then retreated. After a few minutes he made another attempt in a different place and this time he got through. He crossed the flats rapidly, as though there were a prize for a quick finish, and was soon lost to view under the low cliff.

I was beginning to feel hungry now and decided to have some food before I finished the carrying. I returned to the waist and settled myself beside the wheelbarrow to picnic. I saw no more of the cross-channel walker but several of the people who had been landed by *Tern* had come into view. A young couple were climbing to the cairn on the top of North Hill, and a man on his own was having lunch in the bracken beside the winding cliff path that led from the landing beach, and a woman, also by herself, was coming slowly in my direction. As she drew nearer I realized that it was the girl I'd talked to in the bar the night before. She was wearing a bright scarf round her hair and was carrying a canvas hold-all. She came to a stop when she reached me and said "Hullo!" with a friendliness that quite surprised me.

"Hullo!" I said. "So you managed to get away from St. Mary's after all?"

"Yes, I simply had to. I'm afraid I'm not very popular, but I knew if I heard the word income tax once more I should scream."

"Are the sleuths still at work?"

"Yes—they've all gone to lunch with some local bigwig. It looks as though the story's going to drag on for several days yet. . . ." She stood a little uncertainly, holding her bag.

"Won't you join me?" I said. "Have some bread and cheese!"

"That's all right; thanks—I've got some sandwiches." She settled herself on the grass beside me and fished out a paper packet and a vacuum flask. "How have you been getting on?"

"I've had rather a lazy morning, as a matter of fact. I've disposed my belongings and pitched the tent, and that's about all."

She looked around. "Where is the tent?"

I pointed up the hill to the ruined cottage.

"What a good idea! This wind's a bit wearing, isn't it? I'm not surprised the people who lived here found it too exposed."

"It must have been a hard life from every point of view," I said. "The water supply wasn't good and they could only get on and off the island in fine weather and there could never have been much pasture. But what finished them, you know, was a wreck—they lost nineteen men and boys in a ship that hit the Wolf Rock and they never really got over it."

"I should think not—what a terrible thing!" She glanced at the pile of gear. "Is this where you're going to dig?"

"About here, yes."

She studied the featureless surface of the waist. "An archaeologist has to have a lot of faith, I see."

"It's not quite as unpromising as it looks," I told her. "There are sources. The island was called 'the island of St. Samson' in a papal bull of 1193 and there's not much doubt that he lived here. There are several accounts of the ruins of a chapel on the waist at the foot of South Hill, which is where we are now, and they seem to have been still visible as late as 1910."

"I suppose the sand blew in and covered them over?"

"Either that or the stone was taken away for new building—that's what generally happens. But the foundations may still be intact."

26

"How will you set about looking for them?"

"We'll drive a trench across the waist and hope to strike some masonry. If we don't have any luck with it, and there's still time left, we'll dig another trench in a different place. As there aren't any surface indications, it's the only way."

"It sounds as though it's going to be terribly hard work."

"Oh, it'll be hard work, but people who've dug in the islands before have found it very rewarding."

"You mean they've actually discovered things?"

"Indeed they have—bits of pottery and tools and weapons and old stone querns for grinding corn and spindles for weaving. We really know quite a lot about the way people lived here three thousand years ago. Not as much as we shall, of course—there's an immense amount of work still to be done—but little by little the clues are being pieced together."

"You have to be quite a detective, by the sound of it."

"Well, yes—you have to be methodical and observant, otherwise you can easily do more harm than good; and up to a point you have to be able to interpret what you find. I don't claim to be all those things myself, but that's the aim."

"What about these saints—has anything actually been discovered about them?"

"A certain amount. Some foundations were mapped on St. Helen's during the war—that's an island between Tresco and St. Martin's—that definitely suggested a small Celtic church with three circular cells round it. As a matter of fact, that particular site is regarded as one of the most important in the country for throwing light on the history of the Dark Ages."

"And you're hoping to find an equally important one,

I suppose? I can see the fascination of it." She sounded genuinely interested.

"If you're keen on antiquities," I said, "you ought to have a good look round Samson—it's full of them. Have you seen the entrance graves on North Hill?"

"No, I haven't seen anything yet."

"Well, you oughtn't to miss those—they're very fine. Look, would you like me to show you the way? It's a bit rough, but it's worth it."

"Are you sure you can spare the time?"

"Lord, yes—I've got time on my hands till my friend George shows up."

"Then I'd love to see them."

She parked her things at the dump and I led the way across the waist toward North Hill. As we walked I gave her some of the background stuff—how the Scillies had been colonized around 1500 B.C. by a people who had buried their dead in passage graves with stone walls and stone roofs, and covered them with earth barrows, and about the theory that Scilly had had some special sanctification as a burial place, which might account for the tremendous concentration of these tombs in so small a place. I'd just about got to the end of my story when we reached the ridge of the hill and I showed her the open tomb crossed by a large flat capstone that was excavated by Hencken in 1912 and another one not far away in which some incompletely burned human bones had been found. She was fascinated by the rectangular granite box with its end slabs fitting neatly into grooves in the side pieces of granite.

"It seems incredible that primitive people could have made a thing like that," she said; "How do you suppose they managed to work the stone?"

"Probably the same way as the men who built the

Pyramids. They used to make little holes in the stone at intervals and drive in wooden wedges, and then they soaked the wood and it swelled and the stone split."

"Most ingenious!" she said.

We pottered around for quite a while, and when we'd seen all there was to be seen we sat down on a grassy slope out of the wind and went on talking. At least, I did. It was a long while since I'd been so loquacious about my private passion but she kept asking questions and drawing me out. Her curiosity was intense, and I suppose I found it rather flattering. Anyhow, we covered a lot of archaeological ground and had got around, I remember, to the discovery of the site of Troy when she suddenly glanced at her watch and sprang to her feet.

"Heavens, it's three o'clock, and Barney told us all to be at the beach at a quarter to if we wanted to be picked up."

"The boat may be late," I said. "Let's see if we can see it."

We climbed to the top of the hill again and looked down across the hazy channel. I soon spotted the Randall launch. It wasn't *Tern*—it was the new one, *Seagull*, with Jim at the wheel. Through the glasses I could just make out the lanky figure of the cross-channel hiker, standing in the bows. The boat had evidently been in to the landing beach, and was now on its way to Tresco.

"Never mind," I said, "they'll collect you at five o'clock on their way home."

"I know," she said dismally, "but I'd planned to go on to Tresco and stay there for a night or two. What an idiot I am! Now it'll be income tax for dinner again!"

"I'm terribly sorry," I said. "I'm afraid it was entirely my fault."

"Of course it wasn't." She smiled at me, and added,

"Anyway, it doesn't matter a bit. I've had a lovely afternoon and I can go to Tresco tomorrow."

I still felt guilty. "Suppose we go up to the camp and I'll make you some tea?"

"That's a wonderful idea," she said.

We walked slowly back to the tent in the warm sunshine. I lit the paraffin stove and boiled the kettle and we had tea outside on the grass. Afterward we strolled to the top of South Hill. The time passed so pleasantly that I felt quite sorry when half past four came round and we had to set off back to the landing beach.

There were no other people there—the three who had come ashore with the girl in the morning had evidently been taken off in the afternoon. We sat down on the sand to wait for *Seagull*. Several other boats went by, well over toward the Tresco shore, homeward bound for St. Mary's. At last, through the glasses, I made out *Seagull's* green hull. She was following the same course as the others, which seemed strange. It was only when she was almost abreast of us and still showed no sign of turning that I realized she also was heading straight for St. Mary's!

I could hardly believe it. In all my long experience of the Randalls, this was the first time I had ever known them overlook a visitor they had left on an uninhabited island.

We did all we could to attract the attention of those on board. I took off my shirt and waved it, and when that didn't work I climbed to the skyline and waved from there. I shouted till I was hoarse, but the sound simply didn't carry against the wind. The launch continued steadily on its course, and in a few minutes it was just a speck in the haze of the roadstead.

I rejoined the girl, who was gazing across the empty sea with an enigmatic expression on her face.

"Surely they'll remember I'm here and come back for me?" she said.

"I should think so. . . ." I began, and broke off. I'd been trying to puzzle out what could have happened to cause such a slip-up on Jim's part, and suddenly I realized. The Randalls worked by numbers. If Barney had set down four people on Samson in the morning, Jim would have been told to pick up four people from Samson in the afternoon. And that was exactly what he'd done. The man who'd hiked across from Tresco had been the fourth. As far as Jim and Barney were concerned, everything was in order.

And that wasn't the only thing. I remembered now that the girl had said she was going to stay on Tresco. That meant that her husband wouldn't expect her back on St. Mary's; that no one would expect her back.

I said: "Had you arranged to get in touch with your husband this evening?"

She shook her head.

"Is anyone expecting you on Tresco?"

"No. I intended to look for lodgings when I got there."

"Then no one's likely to miss you." I explained about the man who'd walked across. "It looks very much," I said, "as though you're going to have to spend the night here."

3

There was still an outside chance that the Randalls might discover what they'd done when they came to discuss the day's work over a pint, and if so Barney would be back like a shot. Nothing could happen for some time, though, and meanwhile the air was beginning to get very chilly on the exposed shore.

"I suggest we go back to the camp," I said. "It'll be more comfortable there and we shall still be able to see any boat that comes."

She gave another look across the empty roadstead. "I suppose you're right. There really doesn't seem much else we can do."

"We'll try lighting a fire when we get to the tent,

though I'm afraid it won't help a lot. Everybody knows I'm staying here so they'll expect me to have a fire."

"Yes, of course. Oh, well, if nothing turns up we'll just have to make the best of it."

We began to walk back along the path, rather silently. We were both, I imagined, trying to adjust ourselves to an unusual situation, and a slight air of constraint seemed unavoidable. It's one thing to have an interesting discussion with a chance acquaintance in the afternoon and quite another to be thrust suddenly into night-long proximity with a complete stranger. At the back of my mind, too, was the thought that a husband who didn't like his wife to talk to a man in a bar might take a very poor view of her sharing a tent with him on a desert island.

"In the circumstances," I said, as we crossed the waist to collect her bag, "we ought perhaps to introduce ourselves. My name is Lavery—John Lavery."

"And I am Olivia Kendrick."

"Kendrick . . . ? Why, yes, of course, I remember now—I've often seen your husband's name in the *Record*. Ronald Kendrick. Not so much recently, perhaps, but I used to read a lot of his stuff when I was in the Army. He was a war correspondent, wasn't he?"

"Yes, he was in France and Germany."

"It must seem small beer writing about income tax in the Scilly Isles after that sort of excitement."

"That's something a reporter gets used to—at least, he does if he's sensible. No one gets the big breaks all the time. Besides, Ronnie adores the Scillies, in spite of what he was saying in the bar last night."

"He knows them well, does he?"

"Oh, yes, very well. When he was younger he used to come down in January or February almost every year to

33

do a story about the flower marketing. But that was long before I met him."

I could believe that. Ronnie Kendrick was forty-five if he was a day; his wife didn't look more than twenty-six or twenty-seven. I couldn't help wondering what had led such a prepossessing girl to marry a man who was not only much older than herself but was also, to judge by his public behavior, an overbearing, ill-mannered boor. He must, I concluded, have unsuspected qualities.

There was still no sign of a boat when we reached the tent and very soon we stopped bothering about it and got busy with the camp chores. Olivia, who seemed to have reconciled herself to the situation, was anxious to be of use, so I gave her a free hand with the tins of food and the groceries and left her to prepare the evening meal. I spread out the groundsheet in the lee of a wall where we should get the last of the sun and then I went off to collect bracken and driftwood for a fire. By the time I'd gathered a good supply there was a most appetizing smell coming from the frying pan, and plates and cutlery were arranged on the groundsheet with a nicety that George and I were unlikely to emulate.

The fire burned up quickly and made a splendid blaze in the fading light. We sat on cushions of bracken and drank mushroom soup out of mugs and then consumed two enormous platefuls of eggs and bacon. The afternoon's exercise and the novelty of our position seemed to have given us both a good appetite and we ate with enjoyment. Finally Olivia made coffee in a jug.

"You know," I said, as I produced cigarettes and relaxed against a tuft of heather, "this isn't at all a bad hotel. The food's quite good. *And* the service."

She smiled. "You're being very nice to me considering the way I've inflicted myself on you."

"It's no effort," I said, and that was true. She looked lovely in the flickering shadows. More than lovely—mysterious and fascinating. A sudden smile, of course, can alter any face, but I'd never met anyone before whose normal expression was one of cold, almost masklike impassivity and who yet could change it in a second to one of the most alluring charm and warmth. The gap was huge, and each time the charm switched on I felt a shock as though a high-voltage current had sparked across the points. It was stimulating but disturbing, for it was almost like being with two different people at once. There was the same curious ambivalence about her behavior, too—I could see little in common between the cool detachment she'd shown in the bar the evening before and the eager pleasure—almost the relish—with which she had begun to throw herself into our adventure. There were depths here which I certainly couldn't hope to plumb in a few hours.

She insisted on doing the washing up when our cigarettes were finished and afterward we sat by the glowing heart of the fire and talked. Our conversation up to now had been mainly impersonal, but the friendly half light and the enforced intimacy of our situation encouraged confidences. Indeed, she pressed me for information about myself. I told her that I was twenty-nine, and a bachelor, and that I'd been lecturing at University College for nearly four years and quite enjoyed it, but that my real ambition was to attach myself to one of the big archaeological expeditions and that I was making every effort to qualify myself. In return, she gave me a sketchy account of her own activities. As a young girl with a strong creative flair she had become extremely interested in theatrical costume. She'd put in a year or two studying art and had gone on to specialize in period stuff and she'd actually just landed a job as assistant to a woman who was teaching costume in a big art school when, four years ago, she'd met Ronnie. She'd run into him at that haunt of romance, the British Museum, and she'd married him soon afterward and abandoned her career. I expressed mild surprise at that, but she said it had seemed best and I didn't pursue the subject. I observed, not very originally, that a journalist's life must be full of interest and she agreed that it had its moments. Apparently she accompanied Ronnie on most of his out-of-town assignments. I asked her if she ever went sailing with him and she said she'd usually done so in the early days of their marriage but that he was much more venturesome than she was and that lately he'd seemed happier going out on his own. I gathered that when he sailed *Truant* back to the mainland she proposed to travel in the *Scillonian*.

We talked until it was nearly dark and too cold for sitting any longer. Then I broached the subject of sleeping arrangements. "I'll leave it to you," I said. "There's one tent, one sleeping bag, and one air bed. If this were a Hollywood film I should sleep out here and spend half the night making up the fire and the other half doing exercises to keep my blood circulating."

She laughed. "As there aren't any cameras, I think we might both take a chance in the tent."

"Good. In that case you'd better have the bag and the air bed and I'll collect some more bracken while I can still see what I'm doing."

I soon had the tent fixed, with a deep layer of dry bedding alongside the Lilo, and I left Olivia to turn in. While I waited I flung a few sticks on the fire and glanced through the morning papers which she'd brought over with her from St. Mary's. They all carried stories about Scilly, most of them pretty frightful. One drew a stereotyped and quite unscrupulous pen picture of fields golden with daffodils while another, even more imaginative, prophesied an early "mass exodus" from Scilly to the mainland as a result of the tax. I thought of some words of Francis Godolphin, which the reporter could have read for himself if he'd troubled to buy a guidebook—"Yet a very honest man, borne here, may live very happily as many doe, that would not change for twice soe much a year in Cornwall." I frankly doubted if there'd be a single departure. Ronnie's story, I noticed, was factual and restrained, which rather surprised me after his outburst in the pub.

I felt slightly self-conscious as I entered the tent and got down into my bed of bracken, but Olivia was lying still and quiet, and for a moment I wondered if she were already asleep.

"I've been reading the papers," I said. "I must say I give your husband full marks for his piece."

"Oh, yes," she said, her voice drowsy, "he's a good journalist."

I asked her if she was comfortable and she murmured, "Wonderfully." There was a little pause and then she said, "How about you?"

"A bit scratchy, but quite warm. Good night, Olivia."

"Good night."

I lay awake for a while, very much aware of her presence, thinking how extraordinary it was that we should be there together. I could just imagine how George would goggle and exclaim when I told him about it. Ronnie would probably do a bit of exclaiming, too, but it would be Olivia's job to handle him. Meanwhile, everything was wonderfully peaceful. The only sounds were the distant splash of the waves on Samson flats and the low incessant murmur of the wind. Very soon I grew snug and somnolent and sank into a dreamless sleep.

I was wakened by the squabbling of gulls. It was six o'clock, and there was a slanting shaft of sunlight on the tent. Olivia was curled up in her bag with her face turned away from me but I could tell by her deep, regular breathing that she was still dead to the world. I pushed the bracken aside with as little disturbance as possible and stuck my nose out of the flap. The weather promised to be the same as on the previous day—fine, but hazy. I heated some water and washed and shaved, and then I made tea. By the time it was ready my movements had roused Olivia and she soon joined me outside.

The last trace of constraint between us had vanished overnight. It was as though some curious alchemy had been at work while we slept, changing and maturing our relationship, for it now seemed the most natural thing in the world that we should be camping out together on an uninhabited island. It struck me, too, that a subtle change had taken place in Olivia's appearance—a softening, a thawing-out. Perhaps it was because she was feeling more at ease. At any rate, her features in repose no longer made me think of an *aristo* about to make a good end before the *canaille,* and she smiled more readily. At breakfast she was an animated companion, and it was only when I raised the subject of how she was going to get back to civilization that she grew serious again.

"It's a bit awkward, isn't it?" she said.

"It could be. The people here are as fond of a good gossip as anyone else. The only thing I can suggest is that you should wait here until the afternoon boat comes—the one you missed yesterday. Barney and Jim are bound to realize what's happened, of course, but they'll keep quiet if we ask them to, and the visitors will assume you arrived on the morning boat."

She nodded slowly. "That sounds quite a good idea—there's certainly no point in inviting trouble." She gazed down over the water between Samson and Tresco, frowning a little. Suddenly a thought seemed to strike her.

"Where was it that man walked across yesterday?"

I pointed out the approximate route that he'd taken. "It doesn't look possible now, but it's quite easy really."

"Will it be as easy today as yesterday?"

"Easier, because the tide will be lower. The channel should be quite dry about one."

"Then I think I'll walk across too. If this haze doesn't clear, the chances are that no one will see me, and I can find lodgings on Tresco just as I planned. Don't you think that's best?"

I thought of Ronnie, and I had to admit that it probably was.

She said hesitantly, "It's been so very pleasant that I hate making it—well, like an intrigue—at the end, but the fact is Ronnie was really against my coming away on my own at all, only I insisted, and it might look rather odd. . . . Are you sure you don't mind?"

I smiled. "He's your husband—you know best."

"Then that's what we'll do."

The plan went off without a hitch. There were no passengers for Samson that morning, so none of the boats called and we were undisturbed. Shortly after twelve we climbed North Hill and I gave her a detailed briefing on the route across the drying flats to the southern tip of Tresco. Then I went with her to the jumping-off point and we watched the last of the homegoing lunch boats feeling their way through the shallowing channel.

When they'd passed I said, "There you are—it's all yours."

She gave a quick, confident nod. "Well," she said, "thank you for your hospitality—and your kindness."

"If we must be formal," I said, "it was a pleasure."

She slipped off her shoes and stockings and put them into her bag. She looked up at me—and suddenly I realized that I was going to miss her.

"I suppose," she said, "you're not likely to be coming over to Tresco yourself tomorrow? If so, I could buy you a drink."

I hesitated. In the ordinary course of events I probably would have been going over, because I should be needing fresh bread and milk. But in the circumstances I knew I'd better not. I wanted to so much that I knew it would be most unwise.

"That would be fine," I said. "I'll come on the morning boat."

"Lovely. I'll meet you at the inn."

She waved and set off across the flats. When she was halfway over she was no longer an identifiable figure without glasses. She seemed to be having no difficulty in choosing her way and in about twenty minutes she was clambering up the rocks on the Tresco shore.

Rather thoughtfully, I turned back toward the camp.

4

I got down to some serious work on the site that afternoon. Although there was so little to distinguish one part of the waist from another I had in fact noticed a small flat depression close under the hill, an irregularity that could have been natural but might equally have resulted from some earlier activity at the spot. Whatever its origin, it seemed as good a place to drive the trench across as any other. I cut some wooden pegs from bits of driftwood and with a precision that would have pleased George I proceeded to mark out the limits of the proposed excavation, which I'd decided to make about two feet six wide and to take down to a depth of about four feet in the first place. Then I changed into swimming trunks for greater comfort and began to dig. I encountered a few tough roots to start with but as I progressed the ground became easier and by the end of an hour or so I'd dug a considerable hole.

It was monotonous work without company and I felt quite pleased when, in the middle of the afternoon, *Seagull* deposited some visitors on the beach and three of them came sauntering along to the waist and stopped to talk. They turned out to be the man and the girl who had been arguing about moss agate in the pub and the younger of the two men who had been discussing bird watching. The couple were apparently spending their holiday making a collection of unusual stones and they'd been on several of the lesser-known islets to look for them. I promised that if I turned up any interesting specimens I'd pass them on. They were all intrigued to hear about St. Samson and the chapel I hoped to uncover.

"You don't seem to have found much yet," said the girl, peering into the hole.

"Only an empty beer bottle, I'm afraid."

"Those saints undoubtedly knew how to live!" said the birdwatcher. He had a pleasant voice and a most attractive grin.

The young couple strolled off along the beach after a while, their eyes on the ground, and the birdwatcher and I sat and chatted. It appeared that he'd paid his first visit to Scilly only the previous autumn but that he'd become completely fascinated by the teeming bird life and hoped in time to be able to make a modest contribution to the ornithological literature of the place.

"There's always something new," he said, focusing his glasses on the rocks by the water's edge. "See those terns down there. Young Jim Randall told me this morning that as often as not they lay their eggs below high-water mark and have them swept away by the spring tides. You'd think they'd learn, wouldn't you?"

I agreed that they should have had more sense. I asked him if he'd been to Annet, the bird-sanctuary island near Agnes, and he said he'd just managed to get there before the nesting season had started and had got some excellent photographs of puffins. Once he'd started on puffins there was no holding him, and he was so knowledgeable that I felt quite sorry when the amateur mineralogists drifted back.

"Coming, Sutton?" the man called. "We don't want to miss the boat."

The birdwatcher got to his feet. "Well, I hope you'll find the chapel. We'll have to look in again and see what progress you've made."

"You're welcome," I said. "How long have you got here?"

"A couple of weeks—then back to the office desk! Still, it's wonderful while it lasts." He gave a cheery nod and the other two waved and they all went off together, talking hard.

I did two hours' solid digging after they'd gone, and by the time I'd knocked off I'd shifted a ton or two of soft sand and bitten deep into the peaty earth. I'd still found nothing of interest but it was satisfactory to have made a start with the excavation. At least I'd be able to look Olivia in the eye when she asked me next day how I'd been getting on.

I was down at the landing beach in good time on the following morning, a bright, still Sunday, and stood well out on the spit to make sure I should be seen from the Randalls' boat and picked up. As it turned out, *Seagull* had a couple of passengers for Samson that trip—two of

43

the honeymooners who were staying at the Ocean. Jim was in charge and I could hear him going through his patter as the launch approached—"Samson on your left! —and Delilah! The railway station's round the other side!" There were chuckles from the new visitors and tolerant smiles from the old-timers, mostly girls who were sitting up on the foredeck in proprietorial attitudes. As the launch lost way the honeymooners were helped into *Seagull's* blue punt. "I *think* the plug's in, I'm not sure," said Jim. Then a muscular, tousle-haired youth who was evidently one of Barney's "lads" rowed them ashore, carrying the girl dry-shod to the beach on his back and hauling in the boat for me. A moment or two later we were tied up to *Seagull's* stern and I was climbing aboard. Jim gave me a friendly salute and called out, "Have you found the treasure?" and there was more merriment. You make your own fun in Scilly!

The launch was well filled with the usual motley collection of holiday makers in slacks and shorts and wind-cheaters and scarves and mackintoshes, surrounded by the usual clutter of cameras and binoculars and picnic baskets. Once we were under way Jim let the "lad" take over the wheel and began to circulate among the passengers, answering a question here and pointing out an object of interest there. I had often admired his technique on such occasions. "A couple of razorbills over on your right!" he'd call out excitedly, dropping an arm with practiced nonchalance round the shoulders of the prettiest girl in the boat. It was extraordinary how he always seemed to be in the right place at the right time! When Barney was around, Jim generally saw to it that the old ladies got their full quota of charm and attention as well, but today, after a perfunctory circuit of the boat, he concentrated on a dark slim girl whom I'd seen buying postcards in Hugh

Town. He seemed to be making a dead set at her and I rather doubted if Uncle Barney would have approved. It wasn't that Barney was straitlaced but he had a strong sense of professional etiquette and he'd have regarded any serious affair between Jim and a visitor much as the General Medical Council regards a liaison between a doctor and a patient.

The crossing to Tresco didn't take long and in a few minutes I was walking along the quay at New Grimsby, the harbor village, and round the crescent of the picturesque little bay to the Old Inn. I went into the bar, but Olivia hadn't arrived yet. A group of Tresco men assembled there in their best clothes were talking about football, rather gloomily. It seemed that one of Scilly's two teams—I think it was the Rovers but it might have been the Rangers—had just been deprived of its center forward through the inescapable demands of National Service. "We'll be lost without 'e," said one of the men lugubriously. I left them to their sorrow and went out into the garden to wait.

Olivia turned up after about fifteen minutes and she seemed as pleased to see me as I was to see her. She looked fresh and young in a canary-colored jersey and the wind was lifting her dark hair and there was already a slightly sunburned look about her face. She sat down and took the cigarette I offered her and I asked her how she had got on about lodgings.

"Oh, I had no difficulty at all," she said. "I called at the Post Office and they gave me an address at Old Grimsby, just along the road. It's a very small cottage, right at the edge of the sea, but so clean and extremely comfortable."

"So everything went off all right? No complications?"

"No. I rang Ronnie yesterday evening, after I'd got

settled, and of course he assumed I'd already been here for twenty-four hours. It's rather awful of me, isn't it? I ought to feel guilty, I suppose—but I don't. I just feel that I'm on holiday at last."

"Well, that's that," I said, with a slight sense of relief. "Now tell me how you like Tresco."

"It's all I ever dreamed of," she said, her eyes shining. "Have you ever seen such beaches?—and such flowers? I can't think why I didn't come before. Talking to you has stimulated me—I explored the whole south side of the island yesterday evening. I've even got myself a guidebook." She displayed the familiar cover.

"Bring it in with you," I said. "I'm going to hold you to that promise of a drink."

We went through into the long airy bar just as the locals left. It appeared that neither of us had made any firm arrangements for lunch so we ordered some sandwiches with our drinks and retired to a small table by the window.

"So what have you found in the guidebook?" I said.

"Oh, lots of things. I shall have to visit the Abbey gardens, of course, and I'd like to see Cromwell's Castle and King Charles's Castle. They're right at the other end of the island, though, aren't they?"

"Yes, quite close together. I wouldn't say they were terribly exciting."

"Never mind, I'm in an exploring mood—I want to see everything. There's supposed to be a very interesting cave, too, called Piper's Hole. The book says that mermaids used to live there. Now if you could dig up a comb or a beautiful mirror you'd probably be elected a fellow of whatever society archaeologists have, straight away."

"If mermaids did live there," I said, "they must have

had a long flap up on their tails, because it's well above high-water mark."

"Oh, you know it, do you? Is it as difficult to find as people say?"

"It's a bit tricky—you have to know where to look."

"The book says there's a lake inside it and I've never been in a cave with a lake. I'd love to see it."

That sounded very much like my cue. I said: "Well, I've made a start with the trench and I'm in no special hurry to get back. Suppose we go and have a look at Piper's Hole now and we can take in the Castles on the way."

She looked pleased. "Shan't we need a torch?"

"I expect we can fix that."

We had another drink and finished the sandwiches and Bob Frampton, the amiable proprietor, produced a small flash lamp. Then we walked round the quay and set off along the path that skirts the western shore of Tresco. It was warm out of the wind and we took our time, stopping at frequent intervals to admire the scenery. The peaty track, nearly black where the grass had been worn thin, wound its way through dramatic outcrops of greeny-gray lichened granite and magnificent bursts of gorse. There was a wonderful freshness and vitality about everything. New tendrils of bracken were shooting up from the stalky red-brown of last year's growth. The violets were larger than on Samson and the cushions of sea thrift more advanced. Out beyond the weed-covered rocks a few fishing boats and a visiting yacht were almost motionless in the quiet anchorage between Tresco and Bryher. On our left hand there were secluded sandy coves; on our right, steep slopes of empty heath land. It was a heavenly place and Olivia was enchanted. She seemed so happy and carefree that it was hard to believe this was only the second time we'd been together.

Presently we came to a signpost with two fingers, one pointing to the round stone structure at the water's edge called Cromwell's Castle and the other up the hill to King Charles's Castle. As it turned out, the round tower was being repaired—it was festooned with tubular scaffolding and after we'd picked our way delicately over planks we found that the entrance was boarded up. We returned to the path, past a little wooden shed with a fantastically large padlock on the door, and came upon a sunburned man in a white collar and a blue serge suit with a primrose stuck in his buttonhole. He looked like a local inhabitant enjoying the Sabbath. He was sitting on a knoll and had evidently been watching our movements.

"It'll be a couple o' months before she's open again," he said.

"What's the trouble?"

"Bit weak 'ere and there. First time she's been done up."

"Is that so?"

"Yes, and she's not as young as she was. Got to look after these places."

I agreed with a smile. "What are you looking after in the shed—the Crown Jewels?"

He shook his head solemnly. "Cement, wheelbarrer, tools. We 'ad to put that lock on after the old one was bust open."

"Really? I thought everyone was honest round here."

"Round 'ere they may be," he said. "I reckon it was 'ooligans—*visiting* 'ooligans. Didn't take nothing—just broke it open for the fun o' the thing. Shockin' way to behave!"

He nodded amiably and we continued on our way up the hill to King Charles's Castle—a ruin long beyond repair. There was an arched doorway and one intact embrasure and a lot of scattered masonry and that was about all. The view was much more impressive than the monument, for at our feet lay a wild sweep of heather-covered moorland stretching away to the cliff edge. Beyond it we could just see the top of the lighthouse on Round Island. There wasn't a soul about and the only signs of human activity were some galvanized water tanks on the moor and a rotary pump above a well. Presumably that was where the workmen got the fresh water for their cement.

I pointed across the moor to the place where we should find Piper's Hole under the cliff but Olivia seemed in no hurry to get there. She had read that the rocky headlands at the northern extremity of Tresco were particularly fine and suggested that we should work our way round them and approach the cave at sea level. I was in the mood to fall in with any proposal that would prolong our time together so we dropped down the hill again and rejoined the path beyond Cromwell's Castle. Almost at once it petered out, and after that we had to make our own way among steep rocks. It was slow, hard going, but well worth while, for new vistas of cliff scenery continually opened out before us and they were all magnificent.

Suddenly, as we turned a corner and came on yet another striking promontory, Olivia gave an exclamation and pointed to a dark hole in the cliff face. "That's the cave, isn't it?"

"No," I said, "that's a different one—it's called Gun Hole. People often mistake it for Piper's. We might as well have a look at it, though, now we're here."

I didn't expect that we should be able to get right inside because whenever I'd seen it before, even at low tide, there had always been so much water in the deep gully leading to it that the opening had been inaccessible. Today, though, thanks to the phenomenal tide, the entrance proved to be practically dry and the opportunity was too good to be missed. There was no direct way down so we made a wide detour that brought us to sea level at the mouth of the gully. From there, it looked as though it might be possible to reach the Hole by traversing the steep side of the inlet.

Olivia had been happy enough scrambling about the rocks but she gazed rather apprehensively at the heaving water a foot or two below us. Actually I had rarely seen the sea in quieter mood round Scilly, but its oily weight in that enclosed channel was still impressive. I took her hand—it was the first time I had touched her—and drew her along the rocky shelf until the boulder-strewn bed was dry beneath us. There was a narrow fissure that we had to clamber down but that presented no difficulty and a moment or two later we were at the Hole.

After all our exertions it was a disappointment, as caves so often are. It began all right—the opening, seven or eight feet high and shaped like an inverted V on the slant, was quite dramatic. The rough floor sloped up gently for a yard or two, narrowing all the time. Then it descended for a little way and came to an end. There was a deep, motionless pool of sea water that seemed to disappear under an overhanging rock, and that was all.

I let the flashlight beam play on it. "Sinister, isn't it? Can't you imagine the long black arm of a cuttlefish suddenly poking out of there?"

Olivia drew in her breath sharply. She'd been so quiet that I hadn't realized anything was wrong but when I shone the torch on her I saw that she was trembling and pale. "Let's go," she said. "I don't think I can stand it." She sounded quite unnerved.

I steered her out into the sunshine and she leaned for a moment against a rock.

"I'm sorry to have been such an idiot," she said. "I've been in caves before, but they've never had that effect on me."

"I expect it was the pool. A lot of people don't like looking at water in a confined space."

"It had such a horrible stillness." She shuddered. "Let's get back onto the cliff."

I gave her my hand again and we had no trouble on the return journey. By the time we'd reached the cliff top she'd practically recovered—but she'd had enough of exploring. "I think, if you don't mind," she said, "we'll leave out Piper's Hole today."

"What, no mermaids?"

She smiled. "It might be unkind to disturb them. Let's go over there and sit down." She pointed to a ledge of flat rock at the tip of the promontory and we made our way to it and settled ourselves in the sun.

We sat there for a long time. It was a wonderful spot, with a superb view of the wild northern end of Bryher and glorious colors of granite and water everywhere, and sea birds to watch, and the murmur of the surging tide always in our ears. At first we talked, in a desultory sort of way, but presently Olivia fell into an abstracted silence in marked contrast to her earlier mood. She seemed to have something on her mind, and once I allowed myself to think about it I realized that I had a good deal on mine, too. I liked her a lot and I was enormously attracted by her and I wished like hell that I'd had the good fortune to meet her before she'd met Ronnie. But there it was—by the next day, probably, he'd be joining her on Tresco and that would be that. Our meeting, I supposed ruefully, would in time become just a Pleasant Memory.

I was about to suggest that we ought to be moving if I were to catch the five o'clock boat back to Samson when there was a startling interruption. All afternoon we had been undisturbed, but at that moment I heard a step on the boulders above us.

We both looked up, and Olivia said, "Heavens, it's Ronnie!"

For a second I thought I must be dreaming. His sudden appearance in that remote spot seemed too unlikely, too melodramatic, to be credible. But he was only too real, and I sensed at once that we were in for trouble. As soon as he spotted us he came pounding down the rocks with a blind disregard of his own safety and almost before we had got to our feet he had reached the ledge. He was breathing hard, as though he'd raced across the moor, and his face was scarlet. There was such fury in his eyes that I thought for a moment he was going to hurl himself straight at me, but it was on Olivia that he turned.

"So you wanted to come away on your own!" he exploded.

Olivia kept her head remarkably well, considering everything. "If you must make a complete fool of yourself, Ronnie, for heaven's sake wait until you can do it in private."

"It's you that's made a fool of me," he shouted—and I caught the smell of whisky. "Do you think I don't know about your cozy night together on Samson? By God, I could kill you!"

There was a short, tense silence. Then she said: "That was a pure accident. I can explain everything. . . ."

"Yes—now that you've got to! You didn't think of explaining when you rang up yesterday, did you?"

"Only because I knew you'd behave like this if I told you. The fact is, I missed the boat. . . ."

"Because you wanted to spend the night with him in his tent."

I'd been trying to keep a hold on myself for Olivia's sake, but that was too much. "Look here, Kendrick . . . !"

He swung round on me. "You shut up, or I'll break your neck."

It wasn't as much of a threat as it sounded, because I was at least as big as he was and anyway he'd been drinking, but he looked quite ready to try. I felt Olivia's hand on my arm. "Let's go. . . ." she said. Ronnie put his own interpretation on the gesture and lost the last shred of his self-control. He lashed out at me, a wild blow that sent me sprawling against the rock face.

I struggled up, boiling with anger. Olivia cried, "John, *don't* . . . !" I didn't actually intend to hit him, not on that ledge, but my hands were clenched and Ronnie evidently thought I did. He took a step backward, caught his foot on something, and lost his balance. He gave a fearful yell, and the next moment he'd disappeared over the edge of the cliff.

5

We both rushed to the side. The cliff face was precipitous and twenty feet below us the sea was creaming over a pool between boulders. As we peered down in horror Ronnie's head broke the surface in a swirling lather of foam. He began to strike out, feebly, as though the breath had been knocked out of him, and it was clear he needed help. I tore off my jacket and prepared to jump but Olivia restrained me.

"Don't, *don't!*—look at the rocks! Can't we get down somehow?"

She was right. There were jagged lumps of granite only a few feet from the bobbing head—if I went in there I should either drown him or split my own skull. I left the ledge and raced down the side of the promontory where the descent was more gradual. Looking for a place to enter the water cost precious seconds but I found one at last and plunged in.

The next few minutes were terrifying. Even though the sea was comparatively quiet the tremendous heave and surge of the swell kept sweeping me against sharp edges of rock. The tide was driving in against me as I swam toward the end of the promontory so that it was all I could do to reach open water—and that was only the beginning of my troubles. Olivia was still standing on the ledge to mark the place where Ronnie had fallen but as I rounded the end of the cliff I found that the face was a bulging overhang and when I closed in I lost sight of her. Then a breaking wave swept me under. When I came up there were foam and turbulence everywhere and a blinding glitter in my eyes from the rays of the sun on the water. I couldn't see a sign of Ronnie and the noise of the sea made it impossible to hear any cries. I caught another glimpse of Olivia as a backwash swept me out, but then I got tangled up in a line of rocks a few yards out from the cliff, crashing from one to the other until I had little breath left. I got through them in the end but I still didn't know whether I had found the pool or not. My strength was failing and pretty soon I knew I should drown if I stayed any longer. I turned and fought my way back to the nearest landing place and I only just made it. When I eventually hauled myself out onto a rock I was so bruised and exhausted that I could scarcely move.

For a while I lay there gasping. Then I heard a cry from the cliff and Olivia came flying down the hillside, her face drawn with fear.

"What happened—couldn't you find him?"

I shook my head.

She stood as though petrified. "God, how frightful! Are you all right?"

"Just about."

"What can we *do?*" Her tone was desperate.

At that moment I didn't think there was anything more we could do. Ronnie hadn't looked good for a long struggle and I knew only too well the battering he must have had. But as I sat and tried to figure out what might have happened it seemed to me that there might be a chance after all. Where he had fallen the tide had been thrusting straight at the cliff, and the foot of it, under the overhang, had been broken and serrated. He might have managed to scramble out of the water—he might be clinging to some bit of rock now, praying that help would come.

"Olivia," I said, "go as fast as you can to the pub and tell them what's happened. Tell them the only chance is to get a boat round here—quickly, before it gets dark. I'll try to work my way round under the cliff and go on looking. Hurry!"

She nodded briefly and rushed off at once up the slope. In a few seconds she had disappeared over the curve of the hill.

I stripped off my wet underclothes and put on my trousers and jacket and then I went down to the water again and began to work my way from rock to rock, keeping just out of reach of the waves. Every few yards I stopped and studied the surface as the foam spread out and dissolved at my feet. I saw nothing, and scarcely expected to see anything unless it was a corpse, but I was determined to get as far round the promontory as I could. In the end it was the overhang that defeated me. There was a face of rock that I could neither clamber round nor see round and I was in no condition to commit myself to the water again. I retraced my steps and climbed over the hump of the promontory and tried the approach from the Gun Hole side, but again I was brought up short by solid rock. It was Ronnie's appalling luck that he'd gone over the edge at about the most inaccessible spot on the coast.

There was nothing more I could do, so I went back to the ledge and sat there, feeling pretty sick about everything. I couldn't really believe that he was still clinging to a rock. The chances were a hundred to one that he was already dead, and when the tide went down his body would be found at the foot of the cliff. It was a somber thought. I couldn't feel any particular sympathy for him, as an individual, because I'd scarcely known him and what little I had seen of him had been far from appealing, but it was horrible to think that I'd been the cause, however indirectly, of his death, and I felt deeply sorry for Olivia. The whole affair was unspeakably ghastly.

The time dragged terribly and I fretted at the delay. It was nearly half past six before anything happened. Then a launch came nosing out of the channel between Tresco and Bryher, followed closely by two more. *Tern* was one of them, and as she drew level I could just make out the figures of Barney and Jim aboard her. The others I didn't recognize. I stood up on the ledge and waved, indicating the spot where Ronnie had fallen, and they signaled an acknowledgment. But knowing where to look was the least of their problems. It would soon be high water now and most of the offshore rocks were submerged so they had to take the greatest care. The launches stayed well out, and even the punts were rowed in slowly. The closer inshore they got, the worse the conditions became, and one of them was soon in difficulties. I saw a couple of its occupants start to bail furiously while the third rowed it back to its parent launch, and I guessed it had cracked a plank. Whatever the trouble, the other punts were more reluctant afterward to come right in and I couldn't blame them. It would have been easy to drown a whole crew. Barney came nearest to the overhang and for a while I watched him studying the rock face through his glasses while Jim maneuvered the white punt. Then the light began to fail and I knew it was all over.

Olivia returned just before dusk. Several Tresco men had come along with her, among them the fellow in the serge suit whom we'd seen at Cromwell's Castle. There wasn't much they could do at that late hour, but having come all the way they decided to take a last look along the water's edge and went off down the hillside.

Olivia said: "It's hopeless, isn't it?" She sounded terribly strained, but considering that her husband had just been drowned I thought she was bearing up very well.

"I'm afraid so," I said. "The search will go on tomorrow, of course, but they can hardly find him alive. I'm desperately sorry, Olivia."

"I hurried as much as I could but the boats had all left for St. Mary's and we had to phone and get them back. . . ."

"It wouldn't have made any difference if they'd come earlier. They did their best, but it just wasn't possible to get close enough in. Look, let me take you back to your lodgings—you really must rest now."

She seemed scarcely to hear me. "The people at the pub asked me how it happened. I—I told them it was an accident."

"Well, of course it was an accident."

"I don't mean that. I told them Ronnie was trying to climb down the cliff and that he slipped and fell."

I looked at her aghast. "What in heaven's name made you say that?"

"It seemed the best thing to do. I thought about it when I was crossing the moor and it didn't seem safe to tell them what really happened."

"*Safe?*"

"Well, people might not have believed it. Don't you see, if I'd told them that Ronnie turned up in a blind rage because he was jealous, and hit you, they'd probably have thought that you hit him too and that that was how he came to fall over the cliff. I simply had to explain the accident some other way."

I was staggered at her naïve duplicity. "But, good God, you can't just make up stories like that. A man's been drowned—we've got to tell the truth."

"But suppose they found out we were on Samson together. They might easily think . . ."

"It can't be helped what they think. We've nothing to be ashamed of and we both know what happened. Of course we must tell them."

She looked blank. "I don't see how we can do that now. We can hardly go back on what I've said."

A wave of anger swept over me as I saw how she'd committed us. "You'd no right to say it. You've probably got us both in a hell of a jam. Why, it isn't even a likely story. What would he be climbing down the cliff for at his age? Birdsnesting?"

She went very white. "He used to be keen on rock climbing. I—I didn't know what else to say. I just didn't want you to get into trouble on my account."

"That was very thoughtful of you, but unless I'm mistaken we shall both get into trouble now."

"I don't see why. Nobody knows what happened except us. If we insist that he tried to climb down the cliff, no one can prove that he didn't."

"You can't be sure of that—everyone carries glasses in Scilly. How do you know someone wasn't watching us from Bryher?—or the lighthouse keeper from Round Island? It's lunacy—anything can happen once you get tangled up in a thicket of lies."

She was silent for a moment. Then she said in a low voice, "Well, I'm sorry."

"I'm sorry, too," I said bitterly. "I'm beginning to think it's a pity we ever met."

She flinched as though I'd struck her in the face. Then she turned without another word and walked rapidly away across the moor.

6

I continued to simmer for some time after she'd gone. It was bad enough that I should have got involved in this squalid, tragic brawl for which Ronnie's explosion of temper was wholly and solely responsible—to be saddled with a lot of dangerous lies as well was intolerable, and I felt deeply resentful. It was only after I'd cooled off a little that I began to see things a bit more from Olivia's point of view and to realize just how unconvincing the truth might sound in an averagely skeptical ear. I couldn't imagine how Ronnie had found out about Samson, but he *had* found out, so there was no reason why others shouldn't do so too. If they did, the fact that Olivia and I had spent a night alone together, and hushed it up, and then met again for a quiet afternoon ramble, might easily seem to add up to an affair. Indeed, it was hard to see how it could add up to anything else. We should be the guilty couple, and Ronnie the wronged husband, and if we breathed a word about a blow having been struck it would naturally be assumed that there'd been a fight and that I'd knocked Ronnie over the cliff. And in the circumstances, that might be held to be manslaughter!

It was an ugly situation whichever way you looked at it. My firm opinion was that Olivia had been utterly misguided to invent a false story, however unpleasant the alternative, but I could see now what had driven her to it—and her action had certainly been well meant. Indeed, considering the shock she'd had and the personal loss she'd suffered it was quite remarkable that she'd given any thought to my safety at all. My reaction must, I realized, have seemed horribly ungrateful. I'd have gone after her and tried to make amends for my outburst but she'd long ago disappeared into the darkness.

I saw nothing more of the Tresco men, and presently I gathered up my belongings and set off across the moor to the pub. The last thing I wanted to do was to answer questions, but I knew it would be thought strange if I didn't look in at the inn after what had happened. Besides, I should have to borrow a boat from someone now that the ordinary launch services had finished, and the pub was the best place to arrange it.

I approached the lighted door with a certain amount of apprehension. I could tell from the excited chatter that there was a fair crowd in the bar and I had no idea what sort of reception I might get. If by any chance the truth about Olivia's stay on Samson had leaked out, or if Ronnie had given any overt sign of his jealous anger before setting out after us that day, the gossips might already be at work.

As I opened the door everyone turned, and there was a sudden lull in the talk. I said "Evening, all!" with as much assurance as I could manage and there was a chorus of solemn "How-de-do's." Space was made for me at the counter and Bob Frampton said, "Any news, Mr. Lavery?" as he got me a double whisky. I described the abortive rescue attempt at considerable length because it seemed to be the safest thing to talk about. I soon saw I had no cause for apprehension. The atmosphere was sympathetic, even cordial. It seemed that Olivia had told Bob about my swim round the promontory and the story had made a good impression. I didn't know in detail what she'd said, but her version of the accident had been passed around and it appeared to have satisfied everyone. At any rate, I wasn't pressed for fresh facts. All I needed to do was nod and agree with what other people said and tag along.

Presently Bob got me some cold meat and salad and I ate hungrily while the others went on talking. I picked up quite a lot of information in the next few minutes. It seemed that Ronnie had called at the pub during the afternoon to ask if they could direct him to the cottage where his wife was staying—which was how he'd come to hear about our trip to Piper's Hole. Bob had had the impression that he'd been doing a bit of drinking, but apparently he'd been morose rather than voluble, which was just as well. I said I thought he'd been drinking, too, but not enough to make him obviously unsafe on the cliff, and that he wasn't in any case the sort of man you could dissuade from doing anything once he'd made up his mind. Bob was inclined to agree. Everybody thought Ronnie had been pretty crazy to attempt such an exploit but it was clear that no one had any doubts about the story. Reporters, after all, were a queer lot . . . !

I asked Bob if he'd heard what arrangements were being made about searching for the body and he said that one of the constables and a coastguard would be bringing a party over from St. Mary's in the morning. He also told me that the newspapermen had been telephoning for details of the accident and would be ringing again in the hope of catching me, which made me all the more anxious to get over to Samson. Bob said I was welcome to borrow his boat if I didn't mind rowing myself across and I accepted gratefully, promising that I'd be back with it in the morning when I came over to join in the search. His son accompanied me to the quay to show me which one to take and a few minutes later I was pulling out across the channel. By now the ebb was well advanced but there was plenty of water for the punt. A brilliant moon guided me in to the landing beach. The boat was too heavy for me to haul out but it had a very long painter which I made fast to a boulder. Then, reeling with tiredness, I made my way along the path to the waist, climbed to the tent, and turned in.

I woke in the morning little the worse for my arduous swim. I had a few cuts and bruises and I felt a bit stiff but on the whole I had come off remarkably lightly. By the time I'd taken a quick dip and made some tea I was completely restored. It was another splendid day, so quiet and still that the *Scillonian* leaving Hugh Town on her routine run to Penzance looked as though she were sailing on a mirror. I had a leisurely breakfast in the sun and considered my plans for the day. By far the most important thing, I decided, was to seek out Olivia. Whatever her personal feelings toward me, the fact remained that our interests were now inextricably bound up together. Both our futures depended on our story being accepted and that meant that I must know in detail what she'd already said so that I could square my statements with hers. I had a feeling, too, that there were probably gaps and weaknesses that would need attention. It all went very much against the grain, but having once started the story we'd obviously got to make it as convincing as possible.

I rowed myself over to Tresco just before eleven, called at the pub to tell Bob I'd left the punt at the quay, and learned that Olivia was staying with a Mrs. Dean at Bay Cottage. I walked through Old Grimsby and soon found the place. Mrs. Dean, a young, pleasant-faced woman, was packing ixias in a shed at the back. With an expression suited to the tragic situation of her guest she told me that Olivia had gone out for a walk and probably wouldn't be back until lunchtime. That left me in a quandary. I had a little time to spare, for the tide wouldn't be low enough to permit much searching until after midday, but if Olivia had gone off somewhere to brood in solitude there wasn't much chance that I should find her quickly. I walked a short distance along the beach but could see no sign of her and at last I gave it up and set off across the moor to the cliff. The search party was already there, complete with stretcher, and several men had begun to nose about among the rocks at the water's edge. I sought out the constable from St. Mary's, thinking he might want to hear more about the accident, but it turned out that he'd called on Olivia soon after breakfast and for the time being had got all the information he needed. He was glad to see me, though, because he wanted to know just where Ronnie had fallen.

I pointed out the spot and presently, as the tide receded, we were able to work our way round the foot of the promontory to the little rock-encircled pool, which was

65

now almost dry. I felt sure we should find the body among the big boulders between the pool and the overhang and braced myself for the ordeal of discovery—but I was wrong. All we found were Ronnie's big horn-rimmed spectacles directly beneath the ledge—undamaged except for a crack across one lens. The constable solemnly took charge of them.

The search was now extended. The party split into two and began to comb the shore below high-water mark in both directions. It was slow work, for the boulders were slippery with weed and there were many gullies and clefts and pools to be probed, but more people had arrived, including several visitors, so there was no lack of help. I went northward, past Gun Hole and round the corner almost to Cromwell's Castle. On the way back I managed to scramble into the Hole through a foot of water and used up a box of matches making sure that Ronnie hadn't been washed in there. I continued right along, past the gully that led to Piper's Hole, covering ground that many others had covered. But we found nothing more. When the searchers finally forgathered, they had all drawn a blank. It looked as though Ronnie's body had been swept out to sea, in which case it might not be found for days. Indeed, it might never be found.

The constable went off to give Olivia what news there was and I made my way to the top of the cliff. The reporters were standing there, talking to the coastguard, and when they saw me they drifted across. They still hadn't heard a first-hand account of the accident—it appeared that they also had tried to see Olivia on their way in that morning, without result—and they wanted to know exactly what had happened. With some misgiving, I proceeded to tell them. I described how Ronnie had joined Olivia and me on the ledge, and how we'd sat talking together, and how presently he'd said that the cliff looked rather a good climb, and how he'd slipped and fallen, and how I'd searched for him without success. They brought out notebooks and took down my name and address and a few particulars about what I was doing in Scilly, but they didn't seem to want any more details about the accident. I gathered that their interest in the affair was almost entirely personal, because the death of a reporter, even a well-known one, didn't rate more than a few lines in a national daily. They seemed pretty shaken by Ronnie's fate, but they accepted my account without question. One of them already knew about Ronnie's rock-climbing proclivities, which was quite a help.

"If you ask me," said the supercilious man, gloomily, "he ought to have been kept on a lead. I think he was a bit nuts."

"Just eccentric," said the stocky man.

"Anybody who could believe these waters were safe must have been nuts," said the supercilious man. "A chap like that was practically bound to come to grief sooner or later."

Someone else said, "I don't suppose he did believe it. Ronnie couldn't help trying to make an impression. A lot of his talk was—well, just talk."

"He'll be missed in the Street, all the same," said the stocky man. "At least he was a personality, and God knows we need a few. He could be damn good company."

"Yes," said the supercilious man, "for the first ten minutes!" He stuffed his notebook into his pocket. "Well, I suppose we may as well phone a couple of sticks. I don't know about you fellows, but I'm going to tell the office the tax story is dead. I've had this place."

He gave me an offhand nod and the stocky man wished me luck with St. Samson's chapel and they went off in a bunch, looking pretty subdued. I would have liked to get ahead of them, for I thought they would almost certainly make another attempt to see Olivia and I was still uneasy about the unco-ordinated stories she and I were telling. But she'd already talked to the constable, and anyhow my account had been so general that it could be made to fit in with almost anything. In the end I let them get well ahead and it wasn't until after two o'clock that I finally reached Bay Cottage.

Mrs. Dean was in the front garden. I leaned over the fence and said, "Is Mrs. Kendrick about, now?"

She looked surprised. "I'm afraid not, sir—she's gone. She packed up and left about half an hour ago. Mr. Dean's taken her over to St. Mary's himself."

"Oh," I said. For a moment I felt quite nonplused. "What made her decide to go so suddenly?"

"It was when the policeman said they hadn't found poor Mr. Kendrick and didn't know when they would. She didn't seem to want to wait on Tresco after that."

"I see," I said. "Well, thank you very much."

I walked down to the pub in a state of intense irritation. It was natural enough that Olivia should want to get away from the scene of the tragedy, but in the circumstances her deliberate avoidance of me was foolish to the point of recklessness. It might not seem to matter much at the moment, but if suspicion were once aroused the least discrepancy in our stories could be disastrous. She didn't have to be rash, just because she was still angry with me. I decided to go after her and make her see reason.

I had a cold lunch at the inn and then went down to the quay, where the afternoon boats had just deposited their load of visitors. Jim was sitting alone in *Seagull,* looking less ebullient than usual. He asked a few questions about the accident and we discussed the abortive rescue attempt of the previous evening and the fact that the body hadn't been found, which he couldn't understand at all. He didn't think it could possibly have been swept out to sea and felt sure it would turn up before long. We talked for a few minutes and then I told him that I was particularly anxious to get across to St. Mary's right away and he offered to run me over. A quarter of an hour later he put me ashore at Hugh Town.

I made straight for the Ocean and went into the office. The proprietress was there, bent over her books. I said, "Excuse me, but do you happen to know if Mrs. Kendrick is about?"

She looked up. "Mrs. Kendrick? She's left, sir—gone home, I think. She caught the afternoon plane."

7

Well, there it was! I was to be given no opportunity to withdraw my hasty remark—no chance to plead fatigue and temper in extenuation. I was down in Olivia's black books as a man who wished he hadn't met her and she was going to take good care that I wasn't troubled with her company again. I thought her attitude extreme, but I couldn't help feeling a grudging admiration for her pride.

The question now was what I was going to do about it, if anything, and the problem exercised my mind all the way back to Samson. I still thought that for safety's sake we ought to get together over our story, but with her departure the need had become less urgent—she wasn't likely to be making any more statements for a bit. Of course, if Ronnie's body were found it would be a different matter—that would mean an inquest, and we should most certainly have to meet before it took place. But there seemed no likelihood of that at the moment.

There were, in addition, my personal feelings. I wanted to see her again—badly. I wanted to straighten things out between us. But she'd made her position clear and I was reluctant to court another snub. On the whole it seemed better that I should stay quietly in Scilly for the time being and see how things developed.

Once I'd reached that conclusion I fell into a routine that fully occupied my energies, if not my thoughts. Apart from a brief visit to Tresco on the first day to get fresh water and supplies I remained on Samson, walked a little, swam a lot when the sun was warm, and got on with the "dig." I watched the various boats come and go at their appointed times but I rarely went to the landing beach and saw nothing of Barney and Jim except at hailing distance when they happened to cruise near the coast. It was a little lonely in the evenings, but I'd reckoned on a quiet, cut-off life for a week or so and the only real snag was that I couldn't help worrying. I hated the feeling that I was caught up in a web of deceit and I had my moments of sweating apprehension about the outcome of the Ronnie affair. Not that I had any fresh grounds. If there was any malicious talk, I didn't know about it. Each day brought its quota of visitors, sometimes one or two, sometimes half a dozen, and most of them strolled along to the waist and stood watching me for a while, but the only one who referred to the accident was my earlier acquaintance Tony Sutton, with whom I shared a bottle of beer one morning, and he merely thought it had all been shocking bad luck.

The dig was interesting enough to absorb most of my attention. After I'd extended the trench a few more yards

I came across a block of granite which had the appearance of hewn masonry and for a while I really thought that I might have found a bit of the chapel. In fact it turned out to be an isolated fragment and not part of a wall or foundation, but it gave me an exciting few hours while I excavated around it. Soon afterward I cut into a previously undiscovered midden and found some coal ashes and a few bits of seventeenth-century pottery and various bones and an amber bead. It wasn't exactly a Tutankhamen's tomb, but I thought George would be intrigued.

Tuesday morning, the day he was due to arr' /e on the *Scillonian,* opened quietly. As far as I could judge, *Tern* had landed no one at ten-thirty, which suited me well, because I'd planned to do a good morning's digging before going off to St. Mary's to meet the steamer, and I shouldn't be interrupted. Then, unexpectedly, a man came walking along the path. He was wearing a dark suit and a soft felt hat and he looked very much out of his element among the brambles. He nodded a "Good morning" as he reached the excavation and stood watching me while I laid some planks. He didn't ask any questions but he seemed very much interested in the site and the hole and the tools I'd brought.

Presently he said: "Quite a job you've taken on."

I agreed that it was.

"You must be Mr. John Lavery."

"Yes."

"Then I'd like a little talk with you. My name's Field. Detective Inspector Ernest Field, of the Cornwall C.I.D."

I nearly fell into the trench. The absorbing work of the past day or two had lulled my fears, and now that trouble had come it caught me unprepared. For a moment I just stood and gaped at him.

"Mind if I sit down?" he said. He found a soft patch of grass and settled himself comfortably, as though he expected to be there for some time. He was a man of about forty-five, with a long nose and downcast eyes and a general air of having some tremendous secret to himself. I didn't take to him at all. If it hadn't been broad daylight and if he hadn't been so utterly conventional in appearance I should have found him most sinister.

I sat down opposite him, trying hard to conceal my apprehension. I wondered if I ought to express surprise at the fact that he was there at all, but it seemed a useless gambit in the circumstances. They wouldn't have sent a C.I.D. man from the mainland if they hadn't discovered something suspicious.

I said: "What's on your mind, Inspector?"

"I'm inquiring into the circumstances surrounding the death of Ronald Kendrick," he said, gazing at a point somewhere beyond my left shoulder. "I've been told, of course, the version of the incident given by you and Mrs. Kendrick but I'd be glad of your co-operation in clearing up one or two matters."

I hadn't much doubt what *they* were. The Samson affair must have come to light and his other questions would follow from that. He seemed so omniscient, with his calm use of the word "version," that I was tempted to make a clean breast of everything there and then. All that stopped me was the feeling that I hadn't the right to throw Olivia's story on the scrapheap without a fight.

"Go ahead," I said.

"Well, the first point concerns Mrs. Kendrick's movements during the day or two which preceded the tragedy. I've had occasion to make some inquiries about them and I gather that she left St. Mary's for Samson on the Friday morning, ostensibly on her way to Tresco. She didn't return to St. Mary's that night, and I'm told by a Mrs. Dean of Bay Cottage that she didn't reach Tresco until the Saturday. I've also ascertained that she didn't spend the Friday night on any of the other islands. It would appear, therefore, that she spent the night here."

It was a statement rather than a question—a dogmatic conclusion based on painstakingly acquired knowledge. I was a bit surprised that his investigation seemed to have worked toward the Samson incident instead of starting from it, but otherwise things were turning out just as I'd expected.

I said: "Wouldn't it be better if you saw Mrs. Kendrick about this?"

"I should have preferred to, but unfortunately it's not possible at the moment. We don't know where she is."

I was astounded. "Have you tried her home?"

"She hasn't been home."

"Well, didn't she leave an address with the constable before she went from here?"

"She did, but she appears to have moved on. That's why I've come to you for information."

"I see."

I hesitated, but only for a second. He'd marshaled his facts so succinctly that there was no hope here for a rear-guard action. "Well," I said, "I don't know why you're so interested but you're quite correct, as it happens, in thinking that Mrs. Kendrick stayed here that night. She missed the afternoon boat to Tresco and no other boat called here so she wasn't able to leave. . . ." In as matter-of-fact a tone as possible I explained about the hiker who'd walked across to Samson and how the routine of the launches had been upset. "There was simply nothing she could do about it," I said.

"I quite see that, Mr. Lavery, but there is one little

point that puzzles me. Some of Kendrick's colleagues seem to think he was given the impression that his wife went straight to Tresco that day, and that he wasn't informed of this episode at the time."

"She thought it better not to tell him. It was a perfectly innocent occurrence that might have happened to anyone, but we *were* alone here after all, and . . ."

"And her husband might not have believed it was innocent?"

"I wouldn't put it like that, but she did seem to think it wiser not to go looking for trouble."

"H'm! Mr. Lavery, how long had you known Mrs. Kendrick?"

"Known her? I'd only just met her. I'd talked to her in the bar of the Ocean Hotel for about five minutes, that's all."

"And yet she thought it necessary to keep this incident a secret? It sounds as though her husband must have been an unusually jealous man."

"I think he was."

Field looked more secret and sinister than ever.

"So when Kendrick eventually discovered about your night on Samson, which his wife had kept from him, he was naturally very angry?"

That shook me. Field seemed to know everything, and I wished again that I'd seized the initiative by coming clean in the first place. Rather feebly, I stalled. "Who says he discovered about it?"

"Oh, come, Mr. Lavery—I haven't been exactly idle in the past day or two, you know. At lunchtime on the Sunday Kendrick was talking in the Ocean bar to another visitor—as a matter of fact, it was that hiking chap in shorts that you've been telling me about. This fellow happened to mention that he'd seen Mrs. Kendrick on Sam-

75

son and it emerged in the course of conversation that she hadn't been on the boat to Tresco afterward. Kendrick immediately canceled a professional appointment he'd made for that afternoon and rushed off to Tresco and followed you to that place you went to—Piper's Hole."

"Well?"

"After that, according to your—er—version, the three of you had a friendly chat and he then amused himself by climbing down the cliff!"

It was too preposterous, of course. I'd known from the beginning that the rock-climbing story could never be sustained once the facts about Samson were out. And I'd had enough of the inspector's cat-and-mouse act. I took a deep breath and gave him a faithful account of everything that had happened between Olivia and Ronnie and myself from the moment of our first meeting to his accidental stumble over the cliff. It was humiliating to have to admit to a rather idiotic lie, and I suspected from Field's carefully noncommittal expression that the lie had queered the pitch for the truth, but I did my best to make him understand the quite innocent reasons why it had seemed necessary at the time.

There was a pause after I'd finished. Presently Field said, rubbing his long nose, "Can I take it, then, that this second account of yours is the true one?"

"I swear it is. I've told you everything, now, exactly as it happened."

"And although he hit you, you're quite certain you didn't hit him? You used no violence on him at all, at any time?"

"I didn't touch him."

Again there was a little silence. Then Field said: "In that case, how do you account for the blood that has been found near where this quarrel took place?"

8

"Blood!" I stared at him incredulously. "But that's impossible."

"On the contrary," he said, "it's a fact. One of the constables came across it on the Monday afternoon when he was making another search for the body."

"Well, it can't be anything to do with Kendrick, that's certain. I've already told you he fell straight into the sea, and there wasn't a mark on him. It must have come from someone else—some animal, perhaps."

"The blood is human," said Field tersely. "It's fresh, and there's quite a lot of it—enough to indicate a fair amount of damage. If any other person had bled to that extent, I think we'd have heard about it."

It was a baffling development. I said, "Where exactly was it found?"

"On a slab of rock just above high-water mark, at the top of a narrow cleft running up from the sea. About twenty yards to the left of the ledge where you say Kendrick joined you."

"But I tell you . . ." I began—and broke off. The blood couldn't possibly be Ronnie's, of course, but mere repetition wouldn't make the police believe it. Field's assurance was unnerving. I realized now how completely I'd misread the significance of his arrival in Scilly, and how grossly I had underrated the danger I was in. My original assumption that he'd been called to the islands because of the Samson affair had been quite wrong—it was the discovery of the blood that had brought him from the mainland and provoked all his inquiries. And he didn't just suspect me of taking part in and subsequently hushing up a fight which had ended in a fatal but accidental fall from a cliff—though that would have been bad enough. The blood suggested a much uglier possibility, because if Field's description was correct it had been found at a spot where the sort of accident I had described couldn't conceivably have happened.

"Look, Inspector," I said, "let's get this straight. Are you accusing me of doing Kendrick a fatal injury and then trying to cover it up by pushing his body into the sea?—because that's what it sounds like."

"I'm not accusing you of anything," he said, "and that must be clearly understood. If some of the facts seem to accuse you, it's not my fault. All I'm concerned with is to get to the bottom of this business and that's why I asked for your co-operation. The blood is only one of the things that calls for explanation. There are others."

"For instance?"

"Well, the fact that Kendrick's body hasn't turned up. It should have."

"You can hardly hold me responsible for that," I said. "I've always understood that the behavior of a body in the sea is quite unpredictable."

"The local experts don't think so. They tell me that with the wind the way it was and the tide rising, it was practically bound to be left high and dry that night. And that didn't happen." He paused significantly, and I waited for some fresh unpleasantness. "The fact is, Mr. Lavery, I've only your word for it that Kendrick ever went into the sea at all!"

For a moment I just gaped. "What else could have happened to him?" I said.

"Well, there is another possibility, isn't there? As I say, I'm making no accusations—I'm just exploring the various alternatives—but *if* by any chance Kendrick had suffered some fatal injury at your hands the body *could* have been concealed at the top of that narrow cleft—which of course might account for the accumulation of blood on the slab. I'm told it was nearly dark when Mrs. Kendrick got back to the cliff with her Tresco companions, so the concealment would have been quite practicable."

"It may have been practicable, but it certainly didn't happen. It's too fantastic for words. Good heavens, do you realize I damn nearly drowned looking for him?"

"I've been told that's your story."

"And that his glasses were found when the tide went down?" I added angrily.

"His glasses could have been tossed into the sea from the top of the cliff. I'm not saying they were, of course, but they could have been. They're not evidence either way."

He seemed to have thought of everything. I said: "At

least you'll agree that the body isn't in that cleft now? If it didn't go into the sea, what do you suppose has become of it?"

"I wish I knew, Mr. Lavery. It might save a lot of trouble." His glance rested for a moment on the deep trench at our feet, and the huge mound of sand, and the pick and shovel that lay beside the barrow, and suddenly I saw what was in his mind.

"Good God!" I exclaimed, "you can't really think . . . !"

"I'm trying to take everything into consideration. You did have a boat at your disposal that night, I believe? And, of course, you had the tools."

"This is quite incredible."

"It may seem incredible to you," he said mildly, "but such things have happened. Many times—and with far fewer facilities."

The idea was so far-fetched that I was lost for words for a while. My mind went back over the things I was supposed to have done, looking for chinks. "It just isn't a reasonable theory, Inspector," I said at last. "For one thing, if I'd intended to bury his body would I have left a pool of blood on that slab to give me away?"

"You might have. You might not have noticed it in the dark."

"If I was as careless as that, wouldn't you have expected to find traces of blood in other places?"

"Not necessarily—the bleeding might have stopped by the time the corpse was moved. Alternatively, we may still find other traces. Which reminds me—I shall have to ask you to let me go through your belongings."

"That won't take you long—you'll find everything up at the tent. . . ." Suddenly a horrible thought struck me and I had to make an effort to keep my voice steady. "You'll come across some bloodstains on the shirt I was

80

wearing, but they're from cuts I got while I was swimming." I showed him the scars on my arms.

He gave a noncommittal nod. "We shall have to go into that. Perhaps the blood groups will turn out to be different."

"And if they don't?"

"It won't prove anything—but it won't help."

I began to feel terribly depressed. At first I hadn't been able to take his penny-dreadful theory seriously, but the case against me did seem to be building up in a most alarming way. I concentrated again on the improbabilities.

"Look, Inspector, just how do you suggest I moved this body? You say I had a boat, and that's true, but a boat can't get in close to those rocks on the north side of Tresco, not safely. Ask the Randalls if you won't take it from me. In any case, the tide was out all night, which means I'd have had to make my way over a lot of slippery boulders. I couldn't have dragged a big man like Kendrick anywhere near a boat, not over that stuff."

"Possibly not," said Field. "But was there anything to prevent you landing on one of those quiet beaches on Tresco during the night, with some of your tools, and disposing of the body near where it had been hidden?"

"Common sense, I should think. I agree that my position was pretty bad, with Kendrick dead and people quite likely to suspect that I'd got into a fight with him, but it wasn't desperate. If I'd tried to get rid of his body and someone had seen me, I'd have been completely sunk. And that could have happened—there was a brilliant moon and if I'd started rowing around in the early hours or walking over the island carrying a pick and shovel I might easily have been spotted."

"It would have been a gamble, certainly."

"It would have been lunacy. Nothing could have made the risk worth while."

"Nothing?" Field shifted his position and seemed to be making himself even more comfortable. "Mr. Lavery, are you a wealthy man?"

"Far from it," I said. "Why?"

"There's another aspect of this business that I haven't mentioned yet. Possibly you know about it, but for the moment I'll assume you don't. I've had Kendrick's affairs looked into. It seems that since last summer he's been insured under an accident policy for twenty thousand pounds."

That really startled me. "Twenty thousand . . . !" I gasped.

"It's a lot of money, isn't it? An unusually big policy—apparently he arranged it through a broker friend of his. Naturally, it's payable only in the case of a genuine accident—as, for example, falling during an attempt to climb down a cliff! Death resulting from a fight is specifically excluded under the policy. So if by any chance there were marks of fighting on him when he died, it *might* have been worth twenty thousand pounds to someone to bury his body at night."

I took a deep breath. "So I did it for money! Yes, I can just imagine the scene. I, an almost total stranger, have accidentally killed Mrs. Kendrick's husband and he's lying there in a pool of blood. I'm just going off to report it when Mrs. Kendrick says, 'Don't do that—he's worth twenty thousand pounds. Let's get rid of his body tonight and say he fell down the cliff and go fifty-fifty!' Really, Inspector, does that sound likely?"

"It would depend," said Field calmly, "on what sort of woman Mrs. Kendrick is, and what her relations were with her husband—and with you. Until I've seen her and found out more about her, I wouldn't like to commit myself. But I can tell you this—the fact that she lied to her husband about your night on Samson and lied to the police about what happened on the cliff doesn't predispose me in her favor."

"I've explained both those things. And I still say it's out of the question that two strangers could have hatched up a plot like that on the spur of the moment."

"Men and women can sometimes come to an understanding about these things very quickly. Not instantaneously, perhaps—but you had, after all, spent a number of hours alone with Mrs. Kendrick."

"You think she might already have told me that her husband was worth twenty thousand pounds dead, and that she'd welcome an opportunity to collect?"

"It's possible."

"In that case it was certainly a remarkable coincidence that he happened to pick a quarrel with me so soon afterward and at the one place on the coast where the sort of plot you've outlined could be carried into effect. Most considerate of him!"

"I realize you could hardly have known beforehand that he was going to join you on the cliff," Field agreed. "Let's say that it *was* a coincidence—and that, knowing about the money, you took advantage of the unexpected brawl when it occurred."

"At this rate you'll soon be suggesting that I deliberately murdered him. Really, Inspector, you have the quaintest ideas of co-operation!"

"I'm merely trying to clarify my mind."

"Well, while we're on the subject just clarify mine on one point, will you? Surely an insurance company wouldn't pay out on a policy if the body couldn't be produced?"

"Oh, yes, it would—in time. There would be inquiries, of course, but if it seemed reasonably certain that death had occurred, it would meet the claim."

"You surprise me. Well, Inspector, we've covered a lot of ground—perhaps you'll tell me now what you propose to do. Would you like me to help you dig up Tresco, or are you going to arrest me, or what?"

"I'm certainly not thinking of arresting you, Mr. Lavery. The most serious thing I can actually prove against you is that you lied about the cause of an accident. As for the other matters—well, we must wait and see. There may be circumstances we don't know about. Perhaps we shall find another explanation of the blood. Perhaps the body will be washed up after all. Let's hope so. And now, if you don't mind, I'll take a look round your tent."

I got to my feet and set off up the hill toward the camp, with the inspector picking his way carefully through the undergrowth behind me. I was only partially reassured by his last speech. It was true that during the later stages of our extraordinary conversation his manner had suggested that he was testing a hypothesis rather than trying to grill me, but some people might think his hypothesis had come through pretty well. It seemed to cover all the known facts and there was no other theory that did. The evidence was entirely circumstantial, of course, but I had an uneasy feeling that juries had been known to convict on less. I was heavily compromised because of the lie, and if the body didn't turn up and I couldn't think of some other explanation for the blood, things might become extremely awkward. At the very best, I was in for a period of frightful strain and anxiety. And this, I thought savagely, was the moment that Olivia had chosen to do her vanishing act!

As soon as we reached the tent I gave Field the blood-stained shirt. He folded it up carefully and stuffed it into one of his pockets and then he began to go through the rest of my things. His examination was very thorough but as far as I could see he found nothing else of interest and after about ten minutes he announced that he was ready to go.

"I'm afraid, Mr. Lavery, that I shall have to ask you to come with me to St. Mary's. I shall need a proper statement from you about what actually happened on the cliff. I take it you've no objection?"

"Can you guarantee me a safe conduct?" I said rather bitterly. "I imagine these speculations of yours are pretty well common currency by now."

"I wouldn't say that—but I'm afraid there is a certain amount of talk. It's scarcely avoidable in a small place like this."

Gloom settled on me again. Apart from any danger I might be in from the police, it was going to be quite intolerable in Scilly with everyone giving free rein to his imagination. I thought of George, who'd be arriving in an hour or two to start his fortnight's holiday. It wasn't going to be very pleasant for him, either. Still, it was too late to stop him coming now, and I badly needed his moral support. We'd be fairly isolated on Samson, anyway. It was lucky that the reporters had left when they had—though I had a hunch they'd soon be back. A story like this could hardly be confined to Scilly for very long.

We walked in silence to the landing beach. In spite of what Field had said I felt horribly like a criminal in custody and I wasn't at all looking forward to sitting in a launch with him under the curious eyes of visitors. As it turned out, though, I was spared that ordeal for the inspector had hired a boat of his own and it was still waiting at the beach. The elderly boatman showed little interest in me and the quay at Hugh Town had not yet begun to fill up for the arrival of the *Scillonian*. We walked quickly along the main street and a moment or two later I was following Field into the little building that served as a police station. There, in very informal conditions, I dictated my story. One of the constables took it down in shorthand and after he'd typed it out I signed it. That was all. The inspector gave me a nod and said that no doubt he'd be seeing me again, and I was dismissed.

On the way back to the quay I stepped into the Post Office to collect my correspondence. There were several bills and some stuff from the University and three letters, one of them in a handwriting I didn't recognize. It was postmarked Bournemouth, and it was addressed "John Lavery, Esq. Isles of Scilly." It read:

Dear Mr. Lavery,

I am sending this letter in the hope that you are still in the Scilly Islands and that the Post Office people will know how to find you. I hope you will forgive me for troubling you, a complete stranger, but I understand you were present when my son Ronald met with his terrible accident and I wondered if you could possibly spare the time to write to me and tell me just what happened. I am an old woman, tied to my home because of arthritis and very much alone in the world now that I have lost Ronald. He was a much-loved son and I cannot bear to feel that I know so little about that last tragic day. You would be doing me a great kindness.

Yours sincerely,
Caroline Kendrick

It was a surprising communication. Even though Olivia had deliberately gone into seclusion I'd have expected her to get in touch with Ronnie's mother after the tragedy and tell her all about it. In the circumstances there was something rather odd, too, about the absence of any reference to Olivia in Mrs. Kendrick's note. The old lady must have known that she had been there as well. Rather thoughtfully, I stuffed the letter into my pocket. It was going to be difficult to think of a reply and I decided to wait until the situation became clearer before attempting it.

I continued on my way toward the harbor, very much preoccupied, and as I rounded a blind corner I almost collided with Barney, who had just landed his midday passengers and was on his way home to lunch.

"Hullo," I said. It was days since I'd seen him.

"Hullo," he growled. He shot me a surly glance and prepared to pass on his way, but I took a step backward and faced him.

"What's the matter with you, Barney?"

"What do you think's the matter?" he said, in the same uncompromising tone.

"I suppose you've been hearing things about me?"

"I have—same as everybody else in this place that's not stone deaf."

"And you believe everything you hear?"

"I don't say that, but the way I see it, if a man has nothing to hide he's no reason to keep his mouth shut so tight, not with those he's supposed to know."

"If you mean the Samson business," I said, "has it occurred to you that I wasn't the only person concerned? If I could have told you—or anyone else, for that matter —I would have done so, but there were very good reasons why I had to keep the thing quiet."

"Well, it's out now, all right," he said. "Hugh Town's fairly humming with rumors."

"I'm sure it is—and they'll probably get worse. Look, Barney, if you can spare me ten minutes I'd like to tell you my side of the story. I'd be glad of your opinion, as a matter of fact."

With a rather grudging air he came and sat down beside me on the low quay wall and I told him everything. He was slow to respond at first, but as incident piled on extraordinary incident and he saw the frightful dilemma I'd been in he gradually lost his stony look. Of course he was completely staggered and bewildered by it all. The two things most in his mind at the end were the things that were troubling me—the blood, and the disappearance of the body. I had hoped that he might have some helpful ideas about the body, but I was disappointed. All he did was repeat that it *should* have turned up, which I was getting pretty tired of hearing.

"Well," he said at last, "I never did believe the things they've been saying about you, but it worried me a bit. I can see you're in a jam, all right. What are you going to do about it?"

"Ride it out, I suppose—I can't think of anything else to do. Mr. Curtis is due off the *Scillonian* any moment now—he may have a few ideas."

"Let's hope so. I only wish I could be a bit of help—in a way I feel it's all partly my fault. If we hadn't left Mrs. Kendrick on Samson in the first place . . ."

"I wouldn't lose any sleep over that, Barney. The circumstances were exceptional, after all, with that chap walking over as he did. It was just one of those things."

"It was one of those things that shouldn't happen," he said. Clearly he had taken the episode much to heart. "I'll have to think up some better way of keeping a check on people from now on, I can see that."

"You might buy a mobile turnstile," I suggested.

He grinned and pushed his cap back from his forehead with his characteristic off-duty gesture. Presently he went off to lunch, looking much happier. As for me, I was glad that I'd straightened things out with him. Barney was a pretty solid sort of individual in many ways, and it was reassuring to have him as an ally. All the same, the basic facts of my situation hadn't changed, and I couldn't see how they were going to.

I joined the waiting crowd as the *Scillonian* appeared round the end of the quay, and looked anxiously for George among the passengers. He appeared from below as she tied up and a few minutes later he was striding up the gangway, beaming all over his face.

I seized his hand and gripped it hard. "By God, George, I can't tell you how glad I am to see you!"

He seemed pleased at the warmth of my welcome. "Yes," he said, "I expect you've been finding it a bit quiet here on your own!"

9

Now I must tell you a bit about George. In appearance he's a tall, spare man in his early thirties, with an attractively gaunt face lit by a pair of remarkably blue eyes. He has a gentle, almost diffident manner which can be most misleading because being in part an Irishman he's also got a strong streak of obstinacy and intellectual combativeness. He gets his living—and a very good living—with a big firm of construction engineers, working out answers to problems like how much weight a bridge can support before it collapses and how much force is needed to move an object from rest. He's quite unpractical himself—I doubt if he could change a sparkplug without help —but when it comes to applied mathematics he's brilliant.

I first ran across him at a meeting of the Combined Universities Archaeological Society where he was making a characteristically lucid contribution to a discussion about the way the Mayas measured time, and we struck up a friendship which has since weathered several storms. He married, in his early twenties, one of the many women who found his hollow cheeks and slight air of helplessness appealing, but it proved to have been a mistake. The trouble was that he had a romantic, idealized view of Woman and it annoyed him when the reality appeared to him to fall short. I strongly suspect that his vitality's mostly cerebral and that he's really too ascetic for a normal, earthy wife. He can calculate the strain on a metal girder to three decimal places but he was never able to appreciate the stress that Marion was being subjected to by being put on a pedestal and worshiped from afar. Anyway, after a few years the inevitable happened—she became involved in a passionate affair with someone far less remarkable. George, who by his own standards had always been tender and considerate and devoted, simply couldn't understand it. He tried to argue her back with syllogisms but of course it didn't work and in the end she left him for good. He was a bit upset for a time, and so was his romantic view of Woman, but he soon slipped back quite happily into the life of rather erratic independence which he really preferred. It was then that he and I started to spend his annual leaves doing field work together, and this was the third consecutive summer that we'd organized a dig.

Having him there with me now was immensely fortifying and for the first time that day I felt I could bear to face public scrutiny. I helped him stack his luggage against the quay wall and then suggested lunch.

"That's an excellent idea," he said. George is always

ready to eat and yet he never puts on an ounce of flesh. Sometimes I've thought he might be nursing an ulcer but he always seems to be in the best of health and shows no symptoms except a faint irritability·when he runs out of biscuits. He carries biscuits as other men carry lighters.

"I'd better warn you," I said, as we strolled along to the Ocean, "that I'm not terribly popular around here at the moment. If you happen to intercept any dirty looks, just ignore them."

"Oh?—what have you been doing? Digging up something you shouldn't?"

"Very much the reverse," I said grimly. "George, I've got a story to tell you that'll curl your hair, but it's so long and complicated it'll have to keep till later."

He gave me a bright, speculative glance. "I'm all agog," he said—but he didn't press me.

We had a quiet lunch and I told him about the progress I'd made with the trenching, which pleased him. He has one fault as an archaeologist—he's allergic to heavy manual labor. However, he more than compensates in enthusiasm and knowledge. He listened intently while I described the modest finds I'd made in the midden and we had a rather technical discussion about a problem of stratification I'd run into as a result of the activities of rabbits. I told him about the camp arrangements, which he applauded, and we made a list of additional supplies we should need.

"I think," I said, "it might be a good idea if we borrowed a punt now that you're here. I've been managing without, but—well, it's a bit awkward. We'll speak to Barney about it."

"That's entirely up to you, old boy. As you know, I'm not very much good at rowing."

"Practice helps, George! Did you ever try· to calculate

how much energy it takes to overcome *your* initial inertia?"

He laughed. "Tell me, how is Barney?"

"He's flourishing. I'm glad to say we're on speaking terms again."

George put down his coffee cup. "Look, shall we make a move? I don't think I can bear this any longer—I'm on tenterhooks."

We did our shopping and then went straight along to the quay, where Barney and Jim were waiting to greet their afternoon customers. They were sitting on a wooden bench under the wall, deep in conversation, and for once I didn't think it was the wind and the weather they were discussing. Jim looked at me rather solemnly but without embarrassment and we had a lively four-cornered chat while one of the lads went to get a punt for us. Barney offered to take us in the launch with him and tow the punt behind but I said I felt like a bit of exercise. A few minutes later George's things had been put aboard the little boat and I was pulling out across the tide.

We didn't talk a lot en route. It was an enjoyable row, but quite strenuous in the slight chop, and I found I needed all my breath. George, relaxed in the stern, seemed quite content to sun himself and gaze around. It's true he offered to take over when we were four-fifths of the way to our destination but I told him I'd no desire to cross the Atlantic in an open boat and he visibly took no offense.

On the way up to the camp we stopped and had a look at the trench and he renewed his admiration of my efforts. That is one of George's most endearing qualities—he is always appreciative. I showed him my finds and we nosed about a bit around the midden and then continued on our way to the tent. George changed into a pair of ancient flannels and a short-sleeved shirt and as soon as he joined me on the hillside I plunged into my story.

At first he was rather amused, as men are inclined to be when their friends get involved, however mildly, with women. The Samson episode intrigued him enormously. His expression became a bit sardonic when I insisted that my afternoon on the cliff with Olivia had been as platonic as our night together, and I could see that he was expecting to hear of husband trouble. But when I told him what had happened on the ledge he shot upright and stared at me in shocked amazement.

"Good God!" he exclaimed.

"I thought perhaps you might have read about the accident. It's been in all the papers."

"I've been too busy to do much reading. I say, old boy, that's frightful. I *am* sorry."

"That's only the beginning," I told him.

After that he followed every point in the narrative with mounting concern. He was horrified when I told him about my swim round the promontory and staggered at Olivia's lie and vocally sympathetic about my dilemma. His perturbation increased sharply when I got around to the inspector's visit and outlined the case that had been built up against me, and when I told him about the insurance policy that Field had so skillfully fitted into the picture he couldn't restrain himself.

"Twenty thousand!" he echoed, just as I had done. "But that's stupendous. The premium must have cost him a fortune." He looked quite awed.

"He obviously had plenty of money to splash around. Anyway, there it is, George. That's the story."

He gazed at me blankly. "It's almost incredible. God, what a mess!"

94

"I'm afraid it isn't exactly a holiday situation. I did think of wiring you not to come but I left it too late."

"My dear chap, I wouldn't have missed it for anything. It's fascinating. Besides, I should think you can do with some bolstering—you must have been having a hell of a time."

"It has been a bit worrying."

"Worrying! If it had been me I'd have straws in the hair by now." He sat in silence for a moment, pondering the situation. "Of course, you were rather asking for trouble, weren't you?—seeing the girl again, I mean, after that Samson business. What was the idea?"

I smiled. "The woman tempted me!"

"You surely haven't fallen for her?"

"She does rather stick in the mind."

He shook his head. "It's a pity we couldn't both have come down at the same time—we'd have avoided all this. What about her husband—didn't she get on with him?"

"I really don't know—we didn't discuss it."

"I don't see how she could have. It sounds to me as though she was making a dead set at you."

"I didn't get that impression. I thought she was just being friendly."

"She'd naturally soft-pedal to begin with—they always do."

I grinned. " 'Curtis on Women!' " It always amused me to hear George posing as an expert on the strength of one prodigious failure.

"Well, I do know something about them," he said. "Anyway, let's hope she'll soon prove her friendship by turning up and giving you a little backing. Your relationship may have been platonic, old boy, but she's certainly left you holding the baby!"

"She could hardly have foreseen what was going to happen."

"H'm . . . ! Well, let's get back to the main problem —what do we do now?"

"I don't see that we can do anything except wait for Field's next move."

"Really? I'd have said we ought to try to take the initiative in some way. Apart from anything else, there's your reputation to think of—this business could absolutely wreck your career. The faculty would take a pretty poor view if these rumors and suspicions got into the papers."

"They'll take a poor view anyway—something's bound to get in. My statement about what happened, for instance."

"Yes, but that's all mild stuff compared with what Field could give the Press. I wonder if he'll sit on it for a bit. . . . Do you think he really believes in his theory?"

"I think he half believes some of it."

George nodded. "I suppose one can hardly blame him for that. After all, he doesn't know you for the upright citizen you are and there's no doubt he has built up a remarkably ingenious theory." For a moment or two George seemed to lose himself in contemplation of the neat logic which had got me into such a mess. "Everything hangs together so well."

"Including me, the way things are going," I said.

He looked quite startled. "Oh, come, the position's not as bad as that. Field can't get very much farther—it isn't as though he's going to be able to dig up the body."

"I wish I could feel certain he needs to. Do you remember a case a few years back where a steward on a liner was accused of pushing a woman through a porthole? Nobody saw him do it and the body was never found but he was hanged all the same."

"Well, let's not get morbid," said George, though he continued to look a bit shaken. "I'm sure they're going to need more than clever speculation and that's all they're relying on at the moment. Except, of course, for the blood. That's something definite that's got to be explained."

"Easier said than done," I said gloomily.

"I suppose it couldn't be *your* gore?"

"Not a chance. The cuts I got were quite superficial. Besides, as far as I can judge from Field's description I wasn't ever at that particular spot."

"You mean you haven't been there to see?"

"No, I only heard about the blood this morning."

"Well, don't you think we ought to inspect the evidence?"

"I suppose it might be a good idea."

"I certainly think we ought, and I think we should do it now while there's still some chance of finding it. Come on, let's make a move."

I was only too thankful to have some of the responsibility taken off me, and for once George seemed very ready to take it. I could understand why, because this was just the sort of problem he adored. All the way over to Tresco he kept plying me with questions about Olivia and Ronnie, and what each of them had said, and how they'd behaved to each other, and he pressed me for so much detail about the accident that by the time we reached the cliff three quarters of an hour later he knew almost as much about the affair as I did.

There were more people than usual at the northern tip of the island but the promontory itself was deserted. I showed George the ledge from which Ronnie had fallen and the place where I'd gone into the sea after him, and I explained again, now that I could point out the various features, why it had been impossible to locate him from the water. Then we started to look for the flat slab where the blood was supposed to be. It wasn't an easy search, for the colored rocks provided a perfect camouflage except at close range and we had to examine every bit of granite. It was George who came upon it in the end.

The place was very much as Field had described it and I saw at once how well it fitted his theory. Just below high-water mark—or what would have been high-water mark at the top of spring tides—a group of weed-covered boulders enclosed a deep and narrow cleft which continued up to, and beyond, the flat slab, so that a body placed there would have been safely concealed from any casual view. The slab, which had tide marks and marine growth at its lower end, was smooth and dry where the water hadn't reached it. It sloped slightly upward toward the land but there was a little hollow just above the water line where the marks of blood were clearly visible. No doubt Field had removed some of the stuff for tests, but there was still quite a big patch which had dried and turned a dark brown.

"Well," said George after a moment, "your inspector's right about one thing. Nobody could have shed that much blood inadvertently. It looks to me as though someone got hurt fairly badly."

"Anyone might get hurt climbing about these rocks," I said. "The question is, who did? If a visitor had had an accident he'd either have been found here, if it was serious, or else he'd have gone back to the village and had the injury attended to. The same thing goes for a local chap. There'd have been no point in keeping it quiet, and no possibility either. So I'm afraid that's another thing Field's right about."

"H'm! And it isn't your blood. In that case, old boy, it *must* be Ronnie's."

"How on earth can it be Ronnie's when he fell . . . ?"

"He could have hurt himself when he fell, and you didn't see what happened to him afterward. You say yourself that you thought he might have been able to cling to a rock under the overhang, and I should think perhaps he did. Suppose he hung on until the tide got too high, by which time the light would have gone, and then swam round to this spot and managed to climb out?"

"Climb out!" For a second I had a gruesome vision of Ronnie struggling ashore in the darkness after everyone had given him up for lost, crawling inland in the hope of reaching help, and succumbing to his injury in some remote spot. Then I dismissed the idea. On a tiny island like Tresco there weren't any remote spots.

"It's out of the question, George. I'm certain Field has been over every inch of this place. If Ronnie's body had been lying around, it would have been found by now."

"Facts are facts," George said stubbornly. "If that's Ronnie's blood he climbed out. . . . Perhaps he *isn't* dead."

I stared at him. "You mean he may have wandered off without knowing what he was doing?"

"That's one possibility."

"Then where is he? He couldn't have left the island."

"Couldn't he have taken a boat?"

"The loss would have been reported. Besides, he was hurt. . . ."

"Not too badly to move, or he'd still be here. Perhaps, after all, his injury was only superficial."

"We're going round in circles," I said impatiently. "If there was no way he could possibly have left Tresco . . ." I broke off as a thought struck me.

"What is it?"

"I've just remembered—there was a very low spring

tide that night. I suppose he could have got across to Samson or Bryher. For that matter it might even have been feasible for him to walk to St. Mary's across the bar. . . ."

"In the dark?"

"There was a full moon. But it doesn't make sense—wherever he'd got to, he'd have been seen long before now."

"That would depend," said George, "on whether he wanted to be seen. How about that twenty thousand pounds?"

10

George admitted later that he hadn't really given the matter much thought when he threw out that remark and that he only began to consider whether there was anything in it when I started to argue. I suppose that was the Irish in him. I certainly didn't take him seriously.

"You and the inspector should get together," I said. "He thinks that Olivia and I disposed of Ronnie for the twenty thousand and now you think that Ronnie disposed of himself for the same reason. You two could have fun. A regular field day, in fact!"

He didn't even smile. "Well, don't *you* think it's pretty queer? Here we have a man spending heaven knows what on a whacking accident policy, which is a thing hardly anyone does, and a few months later—hey presto!—he has an accident and unaccountably disappears. You must agree it's thought provoking."

"I think it's just a coincidence. From what I've seen and heard of Ronnie's behavior I should say he was accident-prone anyway. Besides, what good would it do him to try to fake his own death? He couldn't collect—not unless Olivia were co-operating with him, and that isn't very likely."

"Is it impossible?"

"I should say it's quite impossible," I said, sharply enough to surprise myself.

George looked a bit huffy. "I'm sorry—I understood you to say you hardly knew her."

"I don't know her, but—well, I'd be very surprised to learn she'd been involved in that sort of unsavory business."

"That sounds like an emotional approach," said George. "What about Ronnie—have you any views on *his* integrity?"

"How could I have?"

"Exactly! The fact is, old boy, you really know damn little about either of these people. Forgetting for a moment that the girl's attractive, can you think of a single valid reason why they couldn't have planned this accident beforehand and involved you because they needed an independent witness?"

"I can think of several. To start with, it was only by pure chance that Olivia and I spent the afternoon where we did, and that Ronnie was able to find out where we were."

George looked thoughtful. "I suppose it *was* pure chance?"

"Of course it was. There was no suggestion of going to Piper's Hole until I got to Tresco that morning."

"Did *you* suggest it?"

"Well, no, as a matter of fact Olivia suggested it, but . . ."

"Couldn't she have arranged that with Ronnie in advance?"

"Hardly! How would she have known I'd fall in with her plan?"

"If she's as attractive as you say," said George dryly, "I'd have thought it was a fairly safe bet!"

He was right, of course. I'd have gone pretty well anywhere with her that day.

"All the same," I said, "Ronnie couldn't have known that he'd find us on that particular ledge, with the high cliff handy and a deepish pool underneath and the overhang to hide him. And the accident couldn't have happened the way it did if we'd been anywhere else."

"Did *you* suggest sitting on the ledge?"

"I imagine so," I said with a touch of irritation. "At least . . ." I made an effort to cast my mind back and I remembered that I hadn't. It had been Olivia who'd pointed it out as a good place to rest.

"You see!" George exclaimed. "Ronnie could have told her about the ledge and arranged that she should take you there. You say he knows the islands well—he's probably had that particular spot in mind for some time."

"Look, George," I said, "this is all very ingenious but I don't believe a single word of it. There was a whole complicated chain of circumstances that brought about that meeting on the cliff between the three of us, and it couldn't possibly have been worked out beforehand."

"You may be right," said George, "but frankly I'm not sure about that. Let's have a look at the chain and see.

Your meeting with Olivia on Samson, for instance—I suppose she knew you were going to be there?"

"Yes, I talked to her about it in the Ocean."

"Did she know you were going to camp out there by yourself?"

"Yes."

"Did she by any chance know you weren't going to have a boat of your own there?"

I looked at him in surprise. "No, I didn't mention that. . . . At least, not to her. I *was* talking to Barney about it. Why?"

"Could she have overheard, do you think?"

"I suppose she might have."

He nodded. "Then I'd say it's perfectly possible that it was *all* planned—not only that she should come over to see you but that she should miss the boat and spend the night with you as well!"

I was staggered. "What on earth makes you say that?"

"I'm just arguing backward from my hunch. If you were cast as a witness of a phony accident, their first concern must have been to make quite sure you didn't suspect its genuineness. Having Olivia stuck with you on Samson for a night would make you feel that Ronnie had a reasonable excuse for rushing over to Tresco and doing his jealous-husband act. I'd say it was essential."

"But they couldn't possibly have arranged that she should be stuck on Samson. The fact that I didn't have a boat of my own is quite beside the point—if it hadn't been for that chap walking across from Tresco she'd have been picked up by the five o'clock launch in the usual way. Besides, her whole attitude . . ."

"I suggest we stick to the evidence," said George. "After all, anybody can assume an attitude."

"Well, as I say, she couldn't have known. That chap walking across was a chance in a thousand."

"H'm! She didn't know he was going to walk across, I suppose?"

I thought back to the conversation in the bar and I realized that she might have known that, too. She'd been standing quite close to me when I'd talked to the hiker about it. Reluctantly, I conceded the fact. "But I'm sure," I added, "that she wouldn't have realized the possibilities —she doesn't know enough about the way the launches work here."

"But Ronnie does—he's an old hand—and if they'd discussed the position that night the point could easily have emerged. And that would account for Olivia rushing across to Samson the very next day—they had to take immediate advantage of a chance that wouldn't occur again. I don't underrate your charm, old boy, but you must admit she was in a bit of a hurry."

I sat in silence, wholly unconvinced.

"There's another thing that ties in rather neatly, too," George went on cheerfully after a pause. "That business of Olivia being on her way to stay on Tresco by herself."

"What's that got to do with it?"

"Why, if she'd been expected back at St. Mary's and hadn't shown up, Ronnie would have been obliged to start a hue and cry and then there'd have been no night on Samson. As it was, nobody had to do anything."

"You're deliberately putting the worst interpretation on every incident. All these things could have come about quite innocently."

"Of course they could—taken separately—but they do rather add up, don't you think? There's another very significant thing, too—the way Olivia suggested that she

105

should slip across to Tresco on foot next day to avoid trouble."

"I'd say that was very natural."

"It may have been very necessary."

"I don't follow you."

"Well, the Samson affair had to be staged in order to prepare you for the brawl, but it would never have done for other people to get to know about your night in the tent. Public suspicion of serious trouble between you and Ronnie had to be avoided at all costs, because there's that clause in the insurance policy that excludes fighting."

For the first time, I felt seriously uneasy. It was uncanny the way George contrived to make everything fit.

"And it was Olivia," he added triumphantly, "who made sure there'd be no talk of fighting by telling that yarn about a rock-climbing accident before you could get your word in. . . . John, we're onto something!"

"Go on," I said soberly. "What else?"

For a moment or two he was lost in reflection. Then he said: "We'll have to go back a bit—there's still one link missing in the chain. When you said 'the woman tempted me,' did you mean that it was Olivia who suggested you should meet again on Tresco?"

I regretted the phrase now, but I couldn't withdraw it. "It *was* her idea," I said.

He gave a satisfied nod. "Then that's that. She got you to Tresco, she proposed that you should go to Piper's Hole, and when you got near Piper's Hole she suggested the ledge. Now the stage is set, and all Ronnie has to do is to make his entry. He arrives on time and puts on a first-class act. He's splashed some whisky over himself to give the impression he's a bit cock-eyed and he behaves accordingly. Having provoked you, he appears to stumble and goes over the cliff into a nice deep pool that he's reconnoitered on some earlier occasion. How's that?"

"Speaking for myself," I said, "the imagination boggles. The sea was fairly quiet, admittedly, but there were rocks all around and he went in backward. If he did it deliberately he was taking a pretty big risk."

"I'm darned sure men have taken greater risks than that for twenty thousand pounds! After all, he could swim—you saw that. For all you know he may be a very good swimmer. Anyway, there's not much doubt he accepted the risk. After that, all he had to do was hide among the rocks under the overhang until you'd finished looking for him."

"Yes, with the sea battering at him!—and he still had to get ashore afterward. Believe me, that's not as easy as you might think."

"I don't think it's easy—far from it. But *you* managed it."

"I hadn't just fallen over a cliff. In any case, there were other risks he'd have had to reckon on besides the physical ones. . . ."

"Such as?"

"Well, for one thing . . ." I began confidently—and broke off as a new and horrid recollection crossed my mind. "I was going to say," I continued lamely after a moment, "that I nearly jumped straight in after him and that if I'd done so any plan he might have had wouldn't have worked because I'd have found him at once. But I remember now—Olivia stopped me. She was afraid I might hit a rock."

"Well, well!" said George. "You know, you've got to hand it to them—they're full of ideas. They thought of just about everything. . . ." His gaze rested for a moment on the patch of dried blood. "Everything except that. If he hadn't bled onto that slab when he climbed out of the water, the chances are the police would never have started making inquiries and the accident would have been accepted by everybody without question."

His confidence provoked more doubts in me. "What about his getaway?" I said. "That strikes me as about the trickiest part of the whole business."

"Well, in the first place he'd have had to know about the low tide and about being able to walk to St. Mary's."

"Oh, he probably knew about that. It was another of the things I was discussing in the pub with the hiker, so if Olivia was listening in, as you seem to think, she could have passed the information on to him. But if he did struggle across to St. Mary's in the middle of the night he'd have been in a frightful state—wet through, bloody, and worn out. Then what?"

George looked a little nonplused—but only for a moment. "Could he have got to his boat?"

That was something I hadn't thought of. "I suppose he could," I said. "There are always lots of punts tied up at the quay."

"Then I should think that's what he did. He'd spend the night drying himself off, cleaning up the blood, and making himself respectable ready for his departure."

"I still don't see how he could expect to do a successful vanishing act. He's not the sort of man I can imagine disappearing—he had a very substantial personality."

"Evidently! But don't you think the more personality he had, the more likely it is that he'd be able to change it when he wanted to. After all, if he could put on that act on the ledge . . ."

"Yes," I said slowly, "I suppose he had some of the qualities. . . . As a matter of fact I remember now he was a good imitator. He did an impersonation in the pub that seemed to go down very well."

"There you are! And didn't you say he had a beard?"

"Yes, a huge beard and mustache."

"Well, he could have shaved those off in his boat—I don't suppose his best friends would have recognized him afterward. Particularly as he no longer had his heavy glasses."

"You're assuming he could see without his glasses? People often can't."

"He could have been carrying a second pair, with different frames. Or he may not have needed glasses at all—perhaps they were a stage prop all the time—plain glass. That would account for them being so enormous. Frankly, I think he had everything laid on for the perfect disguise and I think he got away with it. When did the *Scillonian* sail?"

"He'd have been in luck—she sailed that morning."

"He'd probably reckoned on it. And that would be the end of his troubles. He'd slip quietly aboard, beardless and unrecognized, and at Penzance he'd go ashore and buy some luggage. After that it's guesswork, but I should say he'd register at some previously agreed hotel and wait for Olivia to contact him. Which would explain, of course, why she left Scilly in such a rush and why the police have lost touch with her."

I was speechless.

"And if it weren't for the blood, they could now look forward to collecting twenty thousand pounds and starting a nice, comfortable life together under a different name."

"It's incredible," I said.

"It's a certainty. I'm afraid, John old boy, that you've been the victim of a pretty monstrous conspiracy."

11

From that moment, I can only describe my state of mind as bordering on the schizophrenic. I had been so drawn to Olivia that everything in me revolted against the notion that she could be a scheming adventuress. At the same time the chain of evidence, culminating in that damning bloodstain and Ronnie's disappearance, was so complete that not to accept it seemed almost like a rejection of reason. Instinct and logic were in head-on collision.

I could see the strength of George's case perhaps even better than he could, for there were a lot more things about Olivia that he didn't know or hadn't mentioned and now they all seemed to point in the same direction. I remembered her bored indifference when she had first addressed me in the Ocean bar and her sudden, surprising friendliness on Samson. The change could so easily have been because I'd been chosen as a suitable witness. I remembered her abstracted silence toward the end of our afternoon on Tresco, as though, having exhausted her flow of dissembling chatter, she were waiting for the time bomb to go off. I remembered the provocative way she had caught my arm and said, "Let's go!" when Ronnie had been storming at her on the ledge—an action which might well have been dictated by the need to provide a convincing reason for his subsequent violence rather than by concern for anyone's safety. I remembered her apparent lack of grief over Ronnie's death—explicable enough if she knew him to be still alive. They were trivial points, perhaps, taken separately, but they were all consistent with her guilt.

There were other aspects of her behavior that seemed very strange, now that I came to look back. That odd business of her dislike of caves, for instance. The ostensible reason for our going to the cliff at all had been her eager desire to explore Piper's Hole, yet it had turned out that she had almost a phobia about such places and after all the talk she hadn't even bothered to glance at it. Hadn't the Hole been just a pretext for getting me to the right spot? There was another thing I couldn't get out of my mind, too—the skillful way she'd managed the day's timetable. If there had been a plot, it would have been no use Ronnie arriving at the ledge before the late afternoon because there wouldn't have been enough water below the cliff for him to fall safely. So she'd delayed as long as possible, suggesting that we should walk round the headlands instead of going straight over the moor, exploring Gun Hole with me even though she hated it, and finally settling down on the ledge as though she wanted to spend the rest of the day there. That, at any rate, was how it would look to anyone wanting to complete a case against her.

I didn't mention any of these things to George, for I had no wish to add fuel to his suspicions. Instead, I raised a couple of points that seemed to me to tell against his theory.

"I must say, George, I find it very difficult to believe in a plot that depended for its success on an accidental set of circumstances. Suppose I *hadn't* been camping on Samson, or suppose that hiker fellow *hadn't* walked across. What would they have done then?"

"I suppose they'd have thought of something else. As I see it, they'd got the broad outlines fixed when they came here—they were going to stage a fall from the cliff and have a witness. Once on the spot it was just a question of prospecting for a suitable victim and building a plot round him. The Samson setup was a gift for them, and they snatched at it, but they're obviously an inventive pair and I don't doubt they'd have worked out some other method of compromising you if necessary—or whoever else they'd picked on."

The answer didn't altogether satisfy me, but I let it pass. "There's another thing," I said. "For Ronnie's sudden appearance on Tresco to seem natural, he'd got to make it appear that he'd learned about the Samson affair by accident, through talking to that hiker fellow. Suppose the hiker hadn't been around that lunchtime?"

"I don't think that's much of a difficulty. Ronnie could easily have arranged his day to fit the hiker's. After all, it isn't difficult to keep close to anyone in Scilly."

"Suppose the fellow had happened to have finished his holiday and gone home?"

"Well, there were three other people on Samson with

Olivia that day—any one of them would have suited just as well as an apparent source of information."

I relapsed into silence. I must have looked pretty downcast, because George suddenly said, "Cheer up, old boy. It's hard luck having an illusion shattered but you can't really pretend your life's inextricably bound up with this girl after twenty-four hours' acquaintance. You'll have forgotten all about her in a week or two. And at least you don't have to worry about Field any more."

"You think not?"

"I'm sure you don't. His theory was only dangerous as long as there wasn't any alternative that covered all the facts. Now there is—and what's more it's one that he can easily test. Look, why don't we slip over this evening and tell him the whole story—there's absolutely no point in hanging about. Then by this time tomorrow you'll probably be in the clear again."

An hour earlier I'd have been delighted at such a prospect, but now it left me strangely unmoved. I couldn't even feel grateful to George for the brilliant reconstruction that had changed the whole aspect of things. With the best of intentions, he'd plucked me out of one morass only to plunge me straight into another.

"I think I've done enough rowing for one day," I said. "Besides, I'd rather like to sleep on it."

George gave a little shrug. "Well, I've told you what I'd do, but it's your affair, of course."

It was getting pretty late now and there was nothing to be gained by staying any longer on Tresco. We continued to thrash over the matter as we crossed the moor and by the time we arrived on Samson we'd just about exhausted ourselves as well as the subject. We gave it a rest over supper and soon afterward we turned in. George, who likes his sleep and on this occasion must have felt he'd earned it, was soon dead to the world.

I lay awake, going over and over the treadmill of events in my mind and trying to decide what I ought to do. Of course, I told myself, if Olivia really had been a party to such a sordid and unscrupulous plot, the sooner I stopped thinking about her and turned the whole problem over to Field, the better. There could be no mitigating circumstances—it wasn't as though she was a weak, malleable character. Ronnie's might have been the master mind but she'd been a willing and resourceful accomplice. In fact she'd been quite despicable—if she'd done it. As for me, I'd been a credulous simpleton. I'd succumbed completely to her practiced charm, believing it to be unaffected friendliness; I'd been vain enough to accept that she'd told her tactical lie out of regard for my welfare; I'd even been taken in by her feigned interest in archaeology and had prattled on like a schoolboy. She'd put on a wonderful act, subtle and sustained, and to my lasting humiliation I'd fallen for it. Always assuming that George was right!

But was he? Could one be so deceived in a person one had liked so much? The only answer to that was "Yes, of course!" and I was obliged to put the question to myself more arrogantly. "Could *I* have been deceived in Olivia?" I didn't think so. True, I couldn't swear from my own knowledge that she was incapable of plotting. So much about her was a question mark. I still recalled that strange duality in her behavior which had so intrigued me on Samson, that sense of something unexplained. Undoubtedly she had her secrecies—but that didn't mean she was a crook. I remembered the expression of deep hurt upon her face as she'd turned and left me on the moor. That had seemed genuine, and I couldn't reconcile it with a background of calculated crime.

I tried desperately to think of some other explanation to account for Ronnie's disappearance. If the circumstances had been less rigid—if, for instance, he'd been taking a solitary walk over the island at the time of her vanishing act—I'd have been prepared to believe that someone might have done away with him. His work must have taken him into some pretty queer company, and not all his fellow visitors to Scilly were necessarily what they appeared to be. But no one could conceivably have known he was going to scramble ashore that night, and the idea that some ill-disposed person had happened to be hanging about and had taken the opportunity to dispatch him was utterly fantastic. There seemed no doubt that his disappearance had been voluntary.

That being so, I was brought back to George's chain of evidence. Try as I might I could find no serious flaw in it. Yet I couldn't forget that only that morning the inspector had produced an entirely different chain of evidence on which *he'd* seemed prepared to rely. He'd trusted his logical deductions because he didn't know me and hadn't anything more than logic to go on, and the result had been a farrago of rubbish. Weren't George and I now in danger of making a similar mistake? It had been stupid to suspect me of burying a body in a hole at night—was it any less stupid to imagine that a man like Ronnie, with a good steady job and money to burn, would risk his freedom and his neck for twenty thousand pounds? Wasn't it essential that we should know much more about both him and Olivia before committing ourselves in any way?

For hours I lay and fretted, seeking for loopholes in George's theory, trying to recall a significant remark here, a nuance there, going repeatedly over the rat run of the evidence. When I finally slept, I still hadn't reached any definite conclusion.

I was frying sausages over the stove next morning when George emerged from the tent in an ancient silk dressing gown. As usual at that hour he was physically limp and inclined to be peevish. He pottered around ineffectually, trying to find a new razor blade and complaining that he'd stung himself on a nettle, and he was still in his dressing gown when he sat down to breakfast. It wasn't until he'd got some food inside him that he returned to the subject of Ronnie.

"Well," he said, "have you decided what you're going to do?"

I nodded. "I'm sure you're right that we'll have to tell Field sooner or later, but first I'd like to do a bit of checking up."

"Checking up? On what?"

"I think we ought to try to get hold of some solid evidence before we bring the police into it. Something material to strengthen your theory."

"Isn't the blood material enough?"

"Well, yes, in a way, but there may be other things. Aboard Ronnie's boat, for instance. If he spent several hours there, there may be signs of occupation."

"He'd hardly have neglected to clear up behind him. Still, we could look in on our way, I suppose."

"Also, if he did walk over from Tresco to St. Mary's that night he may have left some tracks."

"Footprints in the sand? They'd scarcely be visible after all this time."

"I know it's a long shot, but I think we ought to look. Then I'd like to see those glasses of his again—they might tell us a lot. And there's another thing that occurred to me—if he really did shave his beard and mustache off that night, the lower part of his face must have looked very white afterward and someone might have noticed when he boarded the *Scillonian*."

"He could easily have got over that difficulty—used some sort of stain, perhaps."

"He might not have thought of it—it's the kind of thing one can overlook. I'd like to talk to the hiker, too, if he's still in the islands."

"What do you expect to get out of him?"

"Well, if it turned out that he volunteered the information about Olivia and Samson and didn't have to have it extracted from him, it would weaken the case against Ronnie quite a bit."

"Oh, come, it's not all that hard to make a person *think* he's volunteering information. Just a matter of steering the conversation."

"I still think we ought to ask."

George looked rather sulky. "Well, I've nothing against making a few inquiries, of course, but I'd have thought all these things were matters the police could go into much better than we can."

"I dare say, but once we've told them our story the whole thing will be out of our hands."

"Isn't that what we want? After all, we did come here to dig."

"I know, but . . . Look, George, I realize you don't see eye to eye with me about this, and you probably think I'm making a complete fool of myself over Olivia. . . ."

"I didn't say so."

"Well, I expect I am, so you needn't hesitate! But it does mean a good deal to me to avoid any blunders. Let's do our best to confirm the theory—we can surely allow ourselves a little time for that." I eyed the gaping trench. "Or, of course, if you'd prefer to get on with the digging,"

I added, "I'm quite willing to make the inquiries on my own."

"No," he said hastily, "I'll come along if that's how you feel. But honestly I don't think it's necessary. After all, there's one absolutely conclusive way to prove our theory, and that's to find Ronnie. I'm convinced it wouldn't take the police long if they once made up their minds to look. And don't forget that you'll continue to be under a cloud until we do tell them."

"I'll survive one more day," I said.

First thing after breakfast we took the punt and rowed round in a slightly choppy sea to the southeastern tip of Tresco, which would have been Ronnie's jumping-off place. I had no hope of a tell-tale line of prints stretching out over a dry expanse of sand toward St. Mary's, because the tides were now only just past neaps and even at low water not much of the foreshore would uncover. The only possibility was that we might find marks near the top of the beach giving some impression of purpose and direction. It was a slim chance, of course, and George didn't attempt to hide his view that it was all a waste of time. He helped me haul the boat out on the sheltered side of the low headland and made a perfunctory inspection of the boulders at the water's edge and then he sat down on a rock and regarded me with an expression of patient sympathy which I found infuriating. I left him there and walked right along the foreshore and discovered a lot of confused prints that had evidently been made by holiday-makers, but nothing of any practical interest. As far as visible evidence was concerned, the question whether Ronnie had walked across or not remained open.

We launched the punt again and I pulled over to Hugh Town. The water in the roadstead was quite rough and George complained of queasiness and nibbled biscuits. It definitely wasn't one of his good days. We were both relieved when, thirty minutes later, we entered the harbor and drew alongside Ronnie's boat. I made the punt fast and we climbed aboard.

At once we had to revise our ideas. Far from having been recently occupied, the little ship turned out to be scarcely habitable. The cabin was padlocked but there were two revolving brass ventilators in the doors and through these we could see that the saloon was piled up with gear—coils of rope, engine tools, an axe, a huge tarpaulin, and a stack of paint pots and cans that almost barred entry. Jim had apparently emptied out the spacious stern locker to give himself elbow room to work on the damaged rudder post, and the contents had been pushed in here and left, I imagined, until Ronnie could inspect the job. One thing was certain—no one could possibly have changed, and washed, and dried clothes, and shaved, in all that clutter. And judging by the dust on the cans, they hadn't been moved for months.

"Anyway," said George, "the boat was only one of several possibilities. He could have rested up in some quiet spot and got dry—in the sort of wind that blows here you dry pretty quickly. Blood dries, too—he could have cleaned himself up sufficiently to get by. He must have done."

"What about his beard?"

"He could have shaved that off anywhere—probably before he left Tresco."

"That would have been no picnic."

"Perhaps not, but it would certainly have been possible. There was a full moon, and there's fresh water in those tanks on the moor and he could have been carrying a razor and a pocket mirror with him. Don't forget he'd planned this beforehand."

George's confidence in his theory was clearly unshaken, and argument seemed useless. Perhaps, I thought, the glasses would help to settle the matter. We got back into the punt and rowed to the quay and a few minutes later we were walking up the main street toward the police station. George looked more disgruntled than ever as we approached the entrance and hung back as though he wasn't really with me and disclaimed all responsibility for anything that might happen.

Field was in the station with one of the constables. He seemed surprised to see me but his manner was no more unfriendly than it had been the day before so I concluded he hadn't thought up any new evidence against me. I presented George, who nodded distantly, and then asked point blank if I might see Ronnie's glasses.

"What's the idea?" said Field suspiciously.

"I'm not planning to destroy any evidence, if that's what you're thinking," I said. "The fact is, we're doing a little detective work on our own. We may have a surprise for you before long."

"I see. Well, it's a bit irregular but I don't know that there's any real objection."

The constable fetched the glasses and I took them from him eagerly. If the lenses proved to be strong it would be a big point in Ronnie's favor, because I simply couldn't believe that a man with very bad eyesight would go jumping off cliffs. I tried them on—and I could see almost as well with them as without! If they weren't actually plain glass, they were the weakest of lenses.

In silence I passed them to George. He put them on and took them off practically in one movement, as though he didn't need to look.

"Possibly a *very* slight astigmatism," he said, "but nothing more." He handed them back to the inspector and turned toward the door. I asked Field if he'd managed to trace Olivia yet, but he said he hadn't. Feeling pretty despondent, I joined George in the street.

We'd scarcely taken half a dozen paces toward the quay when I became aware of quick footsteps behind us. It was such an unusual sound in Scilly that I glanced over my shoulder. It was a woman, and as she drew alongside she stopped.

"Do excuse me," she said, "but would either of you be John Lavery?"

I told her that I was.

"Oh, good—that's saved me a journey to Samson. I'm Monica Dewey, from the *Record*."

My immediate inclination was to tell her that I'd nothing to say, and walk on, but the mention of Ronnie's paper made me think again. That, and the fact that I liked the look of her. She was a woman of about fifty, quite stylishly dressed in tweeds, with a lined, intelligent face and twinkling eyes.

"Have all the newspapers sent down again?" I asked.

"No, we're the only one so far." There was a note of professional pride in her voice. "Our string man in Penzance heard that there were some odd rumors circulating here. . . ."

"To the effect that Mrs. Kendrick and I were marooned together on Samson and that some blood has been found on the cliff and that I made a statement to the police?"

"Something like that," she said, without a trace of embarrassment. "Of course, all I'm after is the facts."

"You mean you've an open mind?"

"A most receptive mind," she said.

I looked at George. "Any advice?" I asked him.

He shrugged. "It's entirely up to you, old boy. You know very well what I'd do."

I pondered. It could scarcely do any harm, I thought, to tell this woman what I'd told Field, because it was all bound to come out very soon in any case. And there was a chance at last that I might be able to get a few questions answered myself.

"I'll make a deal with you, Miss Dewey," I said. "I'll tell you everything I know about Ronnie's death, just as I've told the police, if you'll tell me all you can about Ronnie when I've finished."

She smiled at that and said, "It's a deal, if you're so interested."

"Then let's find a quieter spot."

We walked a little way round the Garrison and soon found a patch of short turf among the gorse bushes where we could talk undisturbed. George, maintaining his pose of critical detachment, seated himself on a low granite wall just within earshot. Miss Dewey produced a thick notebook from her handbag and I proceeded to tell her my story, just as I'd told it to Field. She took it all down in shorthand, quite impassively. When I'd finished she asked me a few elucidatory questions and I answered them without reserve. The whole interview took about half an hour.

"Well, I think that's all," she said at last, closing her book. "And thank you very much indeed."

"As a matter of interest," I said, "do you believe what I've told you?"

"It's not my job to believe or not to believe, Mr. Lavery. But I don't see why not. Of course, there's the blood. . . ."

"There is," I said, "but there'll probably be an explanation of that."

"I think," put in George from the sidelines, "you ought to warn Miss Dewey that if the discovery of the blood

122

happens to get linked with your name in print you'll probably sue her paper."

"Oh," she said, "we're always most careful about that sort of thing. If we report it at all it'll probably be on a different page."

"All right," I said. "Now tell us about Ronnie."

"What do you want to know about him?"

"Everything."

"That's a tall order. He's been a colleague of mine for nearly twenty years."

"Well, first of all, do you happen to know anything about his financial position?"

She looked surprised. "Only that he was always hard up," she said.

I caught George's eye—he had suddenly become very alert. "Really?" I said. "He didn't give that impression while he was down here—he was spending money like water."

"Oh, that doesn't mean anything—he was on an expense account then. I suppose he was drinking a lot?"

"He was."

She nodded. "He always did when he was on a story and could charge it to the office. Sometimes when he wasn't, too—but he couldn't really afford it."

"I always imagined that Fleet Street reporters were well paid."

"They are—and Ronnie certainly was. He used to be one of the stars—I suppose he must have been getting at least two thousand a year at the end of the war and it couldn't have gone down. But he still never seemed to have a bean. . . . He was always very extravagant. . . ." She broke off and gave me a penetrating look. "Why do you want to know all this?"

"I can't tell you—but it's not just idle interest. Do you mind talking about him?"

"Well, *de mortuis*, you know. Still, I suppose it can't do much harm now. The fact is, Ronnie loved spending in a big way. For that matter, he loved doing everything in a big way. He had quite a luxurious flat near Sloane Square and he ran an expensive car and he kept a sailing boat—I expect you've seen it—and he was always buying his wife expensive presents."

"How do you know that?"

"He used to bring them into the office and show them around—bits of jewelry, in particular. He was very proud of his wife. She was much younger than he was, and extremely attractive—but of course you've seen her. He was always talking about her—almost as though he could never quite believe his luck in having married her. Not that he was ever reticent, in any case—quite the reverse. We knew practically everything about his private affairs."

George said: "Did he have any money apart from his salary, do you know?"

"Not recently. His father was pretty well off and left quite a bit when he died—at least, that was the impression Ronnie used to give, though he stopped talking about the family fortune a long while ago. I imagine he went through whatever there was pretty quickly."

"And yet in some ways he was cautious," I said. "You didn't, I suppose, happen to hear about an accident insurance policy he took out a few months ago?"

"Oh, that! Yes, we all knew about that. He bored us stiff with it."

"What did he say? It seems an odd thing to do, for a man who's flat broke."

"It was one of his cranky ideas. A friend of his was killed in an accident in Switzerland and he wasn't prop-

124

erly insured so his wife was left with practically nothing. It seemed to make a terrific impression on Ronnie, and he went straight off and took out that enormous policy. We all thought he was crazy, but he said he was going to make sure that if anything happened to him his wife would be as well off as if he were still alive. Of course, he was always sailing and climbing and doing rash things so I suppose it wasn't quite as idiotic as it seemed."

"He seems to have been a pretty tough character," said George, with an air of innocence.

"Oh, yes, he was—physically very tough. I know that during the war, when he was a correspondent with the First Army, he took a lot of risks that he didn't have to, and he went on doing it afterward."

I was still puzzled about the financial angle. "I can see he lived a very expensive life," I said, "but it sounds queer to say a man hasn't a bean when he's pulling in two thousand a year. By my standards, that's riches."

Monica Dewey was silent for a moment. Then she said: "It's all right until it stops. I'm not sure how much longer Ronnie would have been working for the *Record*."

"You mean he was going to be sacked?"

"Not exactly, because that isn't the way the *Record* does things, but it really amounted to that. You see, although Ronnie was a good reporter he was always making trouble in the office because he was so assertive and quarrelsome. He could be completely calm and rational on paper but an audience seemed to go to his head and he had a genius for putting people's backs up. It wasn't so noticeable in the early years, but lately he'd been impossible. I think it was due to the war—he'd had a lot of headlines and built up a big reputation and when he came back he thought he was a tremendous fellow. So did the office, for a bit. They picked out the big stories for him and he did some brilliant work—there was a black-market investigation of his that Fleet Street still talks about. But he got more and more arrogant and there was obviously no satisfying him and about a year ago he was advised to start looking for a job somewhere else. Of course, he didn't tell us that himself, but it leaked out."

"And did he look for another job?"

"I believe he did, but he didn't find one that suited. The trouble was that he was known all over Fleet Street as a difficult man, so although he was a first-class reporter nobody really wanted him. It wasn't the money—it was simply that they didn't fancy having him around. And of course he drank too much, which didn't help."

"How did he feel about all this?"

"It varied. Sometimes he seemed very down, particularly when it became obvious in the office that he was being gradually edged out. All last year he didn't get any breaks—he was given the dull, unimportant jobs that the newest reporter usually gets, which is pretty galling for an old hand. Some days he'd sit in the Reporters' Room for hours with nothing to do, staring into space and looking as though he could cut his throat—or someone else's! But other days he'd be cheerful and boisterous and boast that any paper in the Street would be glad to have him at a thousand a year more than he was getting if he cared to go, and he'd sound so confident that one almost believed him. Ronnie was a strange mixture—he was certainly his own worst enemy and he could be absolutely unbearable, but on his good days he was a robust and fascinating character." Miss Dewey gazed out over the blue water of the roadstead. "It's difficult to believe that a man like that is dead."

George shot me a sardonic glance. "It is, indeed!" he said.

12

After that there seemed no reason to prolong the discussion, particularly as Miss Dewey was anxious to telephone her story. We walked with her to the main street and then George and I turned away toward the quay.

"Well," he said, "that was a good idea of yours—it's certainly filled a lot of gaps. Now what do you think about the situation?"

I was silent for so long that he lost patience.

"My dear chap, surely there can't be any more doubt? Here we have a tough, wife-proud, extravagant man in financial straits, whose job was folding up on him, and who'd gone out of his way to explain to his colleagues why he was taking out a large insurance policy. Isn't he just the type to try some desperate means of restoring his position and isn't it clear as daylight that he did?"

"I don't deny," I said, "that he seems to fit your theory pretty well."

"I suppose we must count that as progress!"

"But then I'm biased against Ronnie, don't forget. I saw him at his worst—I can believe him capable of pretty well anything—on his own. I'm no nearer persuading myself that Olivia could be a cold-blooded swindler."

"Isn't that simply because you don't really know anything about her? If you were to talk to someone who knew her as well as that Dewey woman knew Ronnie, you'd probably hear a few things that would change your attitude completely."

"I'd welcome the opportunity."

"You're a glutton for punishment, that's all I can say."

"I want the truth. I've got to get this business cleared up somehow, one way or the other. . . ."

We walked on a few steps, while I considered the various courses that were open to me. There wasn't much hope that I could find Olivia herself, if the police had failed, but if I went up to London I might be able to get a line on some friend or relative. . . .

It was then that I remembered the letter from Ronnie's mother which I still had in my pocket, unanswered. I fished it out and reread it. Then I passed it over to George.

From his standpoint, it didn't seem at all strange that Olivia had apparently failed to get in touch with her mother-in-law. "People who've embarked on a secret life of crime don't usually go rushing off to report progress to Mum!" he said. "It's just one more bit of evidence against them. Too bad for the old lady—I'm afraid she's in for a nasty shock."

"I've a good mind to go and see her," I said. "She should know as much about Olivia as anyone."

He looked a bit startled. "You mean go right away?"

"I might as well—I've got to do something. It's no good pretending I'll be any more use down here while all this is on my mind. I'm sorry, George, but that's how it is."

"Telling Field is still the short cut, you know."

"I shan't do that till I'm satisfied."

George regarded me for a moment with a diagnostic frown. Then he heaved a sigh and said: "Oh, well, if it's the only way to get the girl out of your system I suppose you'd better go. It'll be a tricky interview, though, won't it?—if the old lady happens to have read Miss Dewey's piece by the time you get there she may feel like having you thrown out."

"That's a chance I'll have to take. She probably reads the *Times* anyway."

Once the decision was made we wasted no time over the arrangements. The *Scillonian* had already left, so my only hope of getting away that day was to try for a seat on the plane. I rang up at once, and as it happened I was lucky. There had been a cancellation an hour before, and a few minutes later I was booked on the outgoing afternoon plane.

I hadn't forgotten that there were several inquiries I still had to make, and this seemed the moment to make them. The man who usually stood at the head of the *Scillonian's* gangway collecting and inspecting tickets was away with the steamer but I managed to find a harbor official who was generally around when passengers went aboard. He was inclined to shy away at my approach—I suppose he had heard the gossip, too—but I buttonholed him and asked him if he happened to remember noticing any male passenger on the previous Monday week with a peculiarly white chin. He gave me a strange look and said he hadn't. George took my arm and shepherded me gently away, as though he were my male nurse, and we went along to the Ocean for lunch. I took the opportunity to call in at the office there and ask the manageress if the hiker chap was still around. She said he was, but that he'd gone off for the day, so for the time being there was nothing I could do about him.

George was a changed man over lunch. He now regarded my projected trip much as a doctor regards a sea voyage. He was quietly sympathetic about my state and full of helpful suggestions about how I might handle Mrs. Kendrick and about the best way to get to Bournemouth. "You can pick up my car in Penzance," he said, giving me the key. "It'll save a lot of time if you drive."

I thanked him warmly. "I'm afraid this is making a frightful mess of our plans, George."

"Don't worry about that, old boy—I shall find plenty to do. I don't promise to be quite so active as you were— as a matter of fact I rather think I'll go over to St. Helen's and have another look at the chapel there. It might give us a few ideas."

"Don't get into mischief, that's all. No blondes in the tent!"

"If any blonde comes within hailing distance of Samson," he said, "I shall hide in the bracken!"

The journey went very smoothly. I caught the plane immediately after lunch and an hour later I was driving out of Penzance in George's car. It was a powerful machine, very different from the broken-down old thing I'd left in my garage at home, and I didn't hang about. By dinnertime I had covered nearly two hundred miles and was approaching Bournemouth. I stopped at a phone box and rang the number on Mrs. Kendrick's notepaper and a few minutes later I'd been invited to call. I had a meal at one of the more modest hotels and timed my arrival for just before nine.

The house was small and attractive and set well back from the road in a garden of pines. A short plump woman with pink cheeks, black hair and smiling dark eyes admitted me. From her accent I judged her to be German or Austrian. She showed me into a pleasantly lit, chintzy sitting-room where an elderly white-haired woman, walking with the aid of a stick, advanced to meet me. She held out a hand deformed by rheumatism and said, "How very kind of you to come all this way to see me, Mr. Lavery. Now do sit down and make yourself comfortable— you must be desperately tired. Mitzi will bring in coffee at once, won't you, Mitzi?"

The maid bobbed and smiled and disappeared. I helped Mrs. Kendrick to her seat and took the deep armchair that she indicated. Mitzi returned almost at once with a tray and there was a little delay while she arranged an occasional table to the old lady's satisfaction and poured out coffee under a barrage of gentle instruction.

"Mitzi," Mrs. Kendrick said, as the woman was about to leave us alone, "do you think we might have the other bar of the fire on, please?—the room seems just a little chilly."

"Of course—and madame must have her wrap—these spring evenings are dangerous." Mitzi bustled off again and returned with a gossamer affair in wool which she proceeded to arrange about her mistress's shoulders with the utmost care.

"Such a good soul," said Mrs. Kendrick, when the maid had finally withdrawn. "She can't do enough for me. She treats me like a child—but I must confess it's very pleasant to have someone taking so much care of one. Is your coffee as you like it? Poor Mr. Lavery, you must be quite exhausted after that long drive. I am really ashamed of myself for having been the cause of it, but I know you will forgive a mother's anxious heart."

"I was glad to be able to come," I said, "although, to be quite honest, I was rather surprised to get your letter. I would have thought that your daughter-in-law had already told you all there was to tell about your son's accident."

She gave me a sad little smile. "If she had, Mr. Lavery, you may be quite sure I should not have troubled you. No, I haven't seen or heard anything of Olivia. She is very much a member of the forthright younger generation and we all know that nothing can now be done to mend this tragic business. It would be unfair to ask her to share an old woman's grief when she has the whole of her life before her."

I waited in puzzled silence.

"So you will understand," she went on, "how much your visit means to me. As I told you in my letter, Ronald was my only son, my very dear son, and it is a great consolation to talk with someone who was with him at the end."

I felt most uncomfortable—I was not just in one false position, but in several. "It must have been a great shock to you," I said.

"Well, yes—though he was so active and fearless that I have always had to be prepared for something of this kind to happen. But it has left me a very lonely woman. Ronald was such a thoughtful and considerate person, Mr. Lavery. He made me so very happy that it will be hard not to let selfish regrets cloud my thoughts of him. He married rather late in life, you see, and until his mar-

132

riage we lived together in London—such a nice house in Hampstead, opposite the Heath—just he and I and of course my housekeeper. I am, as you see, virtually a cripple. He was so devoted to me. I often urged him to think about finding himself a wife but he always insisted that I came first in his life—as indeed he did in mine. And when at last he did marry it was perhaps not altogether a wise match. . . ." She sighed, and seemed to lose herself in reverie. I began to hope that she had invited me because she wanted to talk about Ronnie rather than to hear about him, but she suddenly said: "However, I mustn't weary you with my sorrows. Perhaps, now, you would be kind enough to tell me about this dreadful accident. A policeman came to see me and he tried to be helpful but he evidently knew very little about what had happened."

For a moment or two I hesitated. I certainly couldn't tell her there was a possibility that Ronnie was still alive, with all that that involved. At the same time, she was so gentle and trusting that the rock-climbing story stuck in my throat. Besides, in a few hours or days she'd be certain to read the truth in the papers or hear about it from someone else. At the risk of being shown the door I decided to give her the bare facts of Ronnie's fall.

"Mrs. Kendrick," I said, "I'm afraid that whatever account you've had of the accident was not the right one."

"Not the right one?" she echoed. She had a very delicate complexion, and now it flushed like a girl's. "I don't understand."

"It came about in quite a different way. While your son was occupied with his journalistic work in the Scilly Isles, it happened that his wife and I became slightly acquainted. On the afternoon of the tragedy we had taken a walk together and were sitting on a cliff top. Your son joined us there and became very angry with his wife. He accused her of infidelity—with me. In his excitement he stumbled, and fell over the edge of the cliff. That is the truth."

For a moment she sat in a shocked silence, staring at me. Then she said: "But I understood it was you who told the police how he had climbed down the cliff?"

Rather wearily, and without much confidence that she would see my point of view, I tried to explain why it had seemed necessary to withhold the truth. It sounded pretty lame, but I made the best case I could. After I'd finished she sat for a while with her head bowed, her hands clasped tightly in her lap. I felt terribly sorry for her. When she spoke, it was in a very low voice.

"Was it Olivia who suggested that you should tell that story?"

"As a matter of fact, it was."

"And may I ask," she said, still very softly, "if there was any truth in my son's accusation?"

"If there had been," I said, "I should scarcely have embarrassed myself by coming to see you. He was quite mistaken."

"I am glad to hear you say that. You seem to me a straightforward young man. I should be very sorry to think that you had been led astray by my daughter-in-law."

"I assure you there was no question of any such thing. Her behavior was impeccable." It seemed idiotic that I should be defending Olivia against a comparatively minor charge when she might well be concerned in a serious crime, but I couldn't help it.

Mrs. Kendrick looked up. "As I thought, you are a kind and honorable man, Mr. Lavery," she said gently, "but I have lived in this world long enough to know that a person who is very anxious to conceal the truth usually has a guilty conscience. You, it seems, were unaware of my daughter-in-law's intentions, and you are naturally reluctant to think her any less honorable than you are yourself. The thing that troubles me is that Ronald, poor boy, was much too infatuated with his wife to behave in that extreme way unless something had greatly upset him— something much more than an accidental meeting between her and a stranger, however unusual the circumstances. If he suspected her of infidelity he may have had reasons we know nothing about."

I was at a loss how to reply to that. "I can only repeat," I said, "that in the short time I knew her Olivia Kendrick appeared to me to be a thoroughly nice and charming woman."

"I am sure you found her so. The difficulty is that one can so rarely judge a person's nature by what is on the surface, and that is perhaps more true of Olivia than of most women. I have often felt that I should never wholly understand her. Poor Ronald, of course, had the same impression as yourself in the beginning." She sighed. "You know, Mr. Lavery, in a way I blame myself for this tragedy. That unfortunate marriage was bound to end in disaster. . . ."

"Unfortunate?" I murmured.

"Yes, indeed . . . As I told you, Ronald and I were very happy together. I see now that we were too happy. Had we been less perfect companions he might have been attracted to the girls of his own class, the daughters of friends of mine, who were so often at our house when he was young. But he always used to say that not one of them was half so interesting to be with as I was, and I am afraid that after a while I stopped protesting. Well, of course, most of those young women eventually married

135

and I think perhaps when he met Olivia he had got rather out of touch with his own kind of people. He had perhaps even forgotten how to recognize a well-brought-up girl. It isn't, of course, anything to Olivia's discredit that she came from some London back street—her father was a carpenter, you know—but these things do leave their mark. A struggle for existence in early life so often makes people impatient with the gentler arts of living, and if opportunity comes their way they grasp it—well, rather greedily."

"At least," I said, "that could hardly be true of your daughter-in-law. Wasn't it in fact the gentler arts of living that did attract her? I rather gathered from her that at the time of her marriage she was finding great pleasure in the creative work she'd chosen as her profession—besides making quite a success of it."

The old lady gave a tolerant little smile. "She would naturally wish to present herself to you in the best light, Mr. Lavery, and if she perhaps exaggerated a little that is only human. Considering her background it is very much to her credit that she was not content to continue indefinitely as a shorthand typist. I feel sure that what she had learned at night school would have taken her beyond the position of—well, of a rather specialized dressmaker—which she was about to fill when she married Ronald. That is, if she had persisted in her studies. But the greater opportunities provided by marriage to an older man are of course very tempting to a good-looking young girl—and Olivia is certainly good-looking. It is no wonder that she has such a fondness for pretty things, for jewelry and expensive clothes, but she was perhaps inclined to forget that Ronald had to work very hard for the money that bought these things."

She pulled her shawl more closely around her shoulders

and I waited for her to continue. It seemed that a taste for monologue ran in the Kendrick family—and uninhibited monologue at that.

"Don't misunderstand me, Mr. Lavery," she went on after a moment, "I was never a possessive mother. I was anxious to welcome Ronald's wife, whoever she might be, as a daughter. I looked forward to being a grandmother. I longed to have Ronald's children here in this house with me—but that was not to be. Again, I don't blame Olivia for not wanting to hurry over these things—children are a great responsibility and do limit a mother's freedom, and though I know my son very much wanted a family he would have been the first to see her point of view. She had led a restricted life and she was young and of course she wanted to accompany Ronald on his assignments and take exciting holidays with him. My son was the kindest and most generous of men—but he has always needed understanding and firm guidance and above all a restraining hand. Olivia, poor child, was not equipped to give him any of these. She was dazzled by him, and—quite unconsciously, I am sure—she encouraged him in just those traits where a woman who truly cared for him would have checked him. I can only suppose that she didn't notice, as I did, the growing anxiety that her extravagance was causing him. It wasn't so important when he still had his father's legacy to fall back on, but capital melts away so quickly these days and although I have always been glad to help him as far as my means allowed I am not a wealthy woman. I know that recently it had grieved Ronald not to be able to give his wife all the things he would have wished, and I cannot entirely forgive her for not realizing the acute unhappiness she was causing him. An insatiable appetite for money is a dreadful thing, Mr. Lavery."

I had listened to her concluding words with growing distress, and she must have sensed my discomfort.

"Perhaps I have spoken more frankly than I should about these family matters," she said, "but it is always easier, is it not, to talk about such things to a complete stranger, and it has been a relief to me to unburden myself a little. I hope you will pardon an old woman's garrulity."

"I am honored by your confidence," I said.

"And now I am afraid I shall have to think about getting to bed—it takes me so long, even with Mitzi to help me." She reached for her stick and started to raise herself from her chair, and I jumped up to help her.

"Thank you, Mr. Lavery," she said, "you are very kind and attentive—just as Ronald used to be. May I say again how much I have appreciated your visit? In spite of the unhappy circumstances it has been a pleasure to meet you —and I am sure you were in no way to blame for what happened. Good-by."

"Good-by," I said.

She touched the bell, and a moment later Mitzi showed me out.

13

I suppose if I'd had any sense, that would have been the moment when I'd have taken the decision to pass the whole affair over to the police. The things Mrs. Kendrick had told me, if true, enormously strengthened the case against Olivia and Ronnie, and even allowing for her obvious prejudice against her daughter-in-law they couldn't entirely be brushed aside. They accorded in too many respects with what I knew from other sources. Whether or not Olivia had deliberately married Ronnie for what she could get out of him, there could be no doubt whatever that she'd proved a most expensive wife. That elegance of hers had had to be paid for, and it was something I'd seen with my own eyes. Miss Dewey, too, had told us of the costly presents that Ronnie was always buying, and of the sumptuous flat and car, so in that respect at least Mrs. Kendrick's account was fully confirmed. There could be no doubt, either, about Ronnie's financial anxieties, for the impartial Miss Dewey had drawn an even more pessimistic picture of his circumstances than his mother had. As for his feelings about Olivia, I still remembered the jealous stare he'd given me that first night in the pub, and I could well believe that the word "infatuation" was not a bit too strong. And those were really all the ingredients one needed. It wasn't difficult to see how an uxorious, middle-aged man, desperately afraid he might lose his lovely young wife unless he could continue to satisfy her exacting material demands, might seek her co-operation in a remunerative crime. It wasn't difficult to believe that a gold-digging wife might give it. When one added to all that the damning sequence of events in Scilly, the otherwise inexplicable blood, and the disappearance of both principals, the conclusion seemed inescapable.

Dejectedly I turned the car and drove down toward the sea front, looking for a hotel where I could spend the night. There were lots of them, all excellent hotels, but to my jaundiced eye they were about as attractive as a morgue. Suddenly I realized that I didn't want to stay in Bournemouth at all. I was tired, but it wasn't the sort of tiredness that a night in a hotel would put right. I wanted to get back to Scilly, if only to talk things over with George. I knew what his reaction would be, but even that would be better than brooding over the situation alone. If I drove through the night I should be in Penzance in time to catch the *Scillonian* in the morning, and by lunchtime I'd be back on Samson.

I filled up with petrol and bought some sandwiches at a snack bar and a few minutes later I was on my way. The road was pretty empty and the car lights were good and I quite enjoyed the long, fast drive. It gave me the illusion of action, which was what I needed. About two in the morning I pulled in off the road and slept for several hours in the back of the car, wrapped in a rug. At dawn I set off again, and by eight I was running into Penzance. I garaged the car and had breakfast at an early café and even found time for a shave.

On the way down to the harbor I bought a copy of the *Record* and turned to see what Monica Dewey had written about me. Her story was shorter than I'd expected and consisted mainly of a few direct quotations from my revised account of the accident. There was nothing about the blood, nor any overt suggestion of what the police call "foul play," but I emerged in a far from favorable light and anyone reading between the lines could have been forgiven for thinking that I was still trying to cover up a fight that had had a fatal end. Still, that wasn't Miss Dewey's fault.

I boarded the *Scillonian* with ten minutes to spare. In spite of all my anxiety I couldn't entirely escape the sense of pleasurable excitement that seemed inseparable from joining the friendly little steamer. I watched the ropes being cast off and the skillful maneuvering away from the quay, and then I strolled along the deck to see if my favorite seat in the stern was free. There wasn't a great crowd of passengers aboard and most of them were at the railing pointing out landmarks on the dramatic Cornish coastline, but the seat proved to be occupied. There was a woman there, sitting by herself. She turned as I approached, and I caught my breath.

It was Olivia!

Even after all this time I find it hard to set down calmly my emotions on seeing her again. I was utterly astonished, of course, and I couldn't imagine what she was doing there, and I felt something like panic as I realized that here and now the showdown was upon me. I had a sick, empty feeling in my stomach, too, because now that I saw her again I knew that I was hopelessly, desperately in love with her and had been ever since Samson and would go on being against all sanity and reason whatever she'd done or hadn't done. It was something out of my power to control, even if I'd wanted to.

There was surprise on her face as well, but it was she who recovered first. After what seemed a moment of doubt, she gave me a friendly smile. "Well," she exclaimed, "this is a most extraordinary thing! I'm actually on my way to see you."

I scarcely knew what to say. My thoughts were in chaos. I wanted to question her, reproach her, appeal to her, denounce her, all in a breath. So much had happened, and there was such a gulf between us, that it was hard to know where to begin. In the end it seemed simpler to take things as they came.

I said: "Where have you been?"

"I've been staying with some friends in Newlyn."

I knew the place. It was a haunt of painters, a picturesque village adjoining Penzance.

"The police have been looking for you," I said.

"Oh, dear, have they? I suppose I ought to have let them know when I moved on. I gave them my address in Penzance but when I got to the hotel everybody seemed to be talking about Scilly and I couldn't stand it so I packed up and went to some artist people I knew as they were practically on the doorstep. I was sure that if Ronnie was found I should read about it anyway."

She was so glib, so assured, it was breathtaking.

I said: "Why this sudden desire to see me?"

"Because of this, of course." She held out a folded copy of the *Record* and I caught the headline over Miss Dewey's story. "I saw it at breakfast and rushed straight off to catch the boat. Haven't you seen it?"

"Yes, I've seen it."

"I suppose you had to tell them?"

"Yes, I had no option. . . ." I struggled to focus my mind on essentials. "I'm still not clear why you've come back."

She looked at me reproachfully. "You don't suppose I would leave you to face this by yourself, do you? I'd never have gone away in the first place if I hadn't felt so stupidly certain that there wouldn't be any trouble. Surely you realize that?" Her eyes held mine with an expression of perfect candor. "I was a fool, John—I can see that now, and I'm terribly sorry about it. I ought never to have landed you with that rock-climbing story and I'm not surprised you were angry. Can you possibly forgive me?"

I could hardly believe that after all that had happened we were right back there. "It scarcely matters now," I said. "The damage is done."

Her face fell. "I imagined you might feel like that. But the damage isn't irretrievable, is it?—surely we can undo it? You've told them now what really happened, and I shall tell them too, and they'll have to believe us. We'll *make* them."

"I'm afraid," I said, "you don't quite realize the extent of the damage. While you've been hiding away, there've been a lot of unpleasant developments. A police inspector has been over, from the mainland, asking questions and nosing about. He can't understand why Ronnie's body hasn't turned up. He seems to think that I disposed of it in some way—and that you helped me. That's why they wanted to talk to you."

143

She stared at me incredulously. "You can't be serious?"

"I'm deadly serious. We're practically under suspicion of murder."

"But . . . Why, I've never heard anything so fantastic in my life. They must be out of their minds. What on earth could have given them that idea?"

"They've found out that Ronnie was insured for twenty thousand pounds. They think we were lovers and that we got rid of him so that we could have the money. You did know about the money, I suppose?"

"Of course I knew, but . . . How utterly preposterous! You're surely not worried about it, are you?—they can't possibly have any evidence."

"On the contrary," I said, "they have a great deal of evidence. You're a little out of touch with events. Among other things, they've discovered a pool of blood on a rock just above the sea."

"Blood!"

"Yes." I told her about the slab. "And they've decided it's Ronnie's blood."

"But it couldn't possibly be. . . ."

"It could be, and I think it is. If he was injured in the sea, and climbed out onto the rock . . ."

She turned very pale and suddenly she swayed in her seat, so that I thought she was going to faint and had to hold her.

I felt pretty sick myself. If she'd signed a written confession of guilt she could hardly have given herself away more completely.

14

The faintness gradually passed but she still looked badly shaken. She sat for a while with her face slightly turned away, gazing out over the sea. Then she began to fumble in her handbag.

"I thought that might be a bit of a shock for you," I said.

"I'm all right now. . . . I suddenly had a picture of Ronnie lying out there on a rock in the darkness, hurt and bleeding. . . ." She looked at me miserably. "I suppose he must have struggled out somehow and then slipped back into the sea? God, what a ghastly end! It was bad enough to think he'd been drowned straight away—but he may have been there for hours. And if we'd only known we might have saved him."

If it was a performance, it was superb.

I sat down beside her, determined not to let this go on any longer. "There's a school of thought, Olivia, that holds it's possible Ronnie didn't slip back into the sea."

She stared at me, her eyes huge against the pallor of her cheeks. "What on earth do you mean?"

I forced myself to tell her. I had made up my mind that if this moment ever came and I had to present the case against her I would be cool and detached and not humiliate myself by letting her see how much it all meant to me, but now that I was actually putting the incredible accusation into words I found myself trembling and could scarcely control my voice.

She sat watching me, taut and motionless, while I recalled the succession of incidents on St. Mary's and Samson and Tresco that fitted so neatly into the pattern of a skillfully engineered plot. I covered all the ground in detail, and it took a long while. Throughout, she didn't say a word—she just listened, attentive and expressionless.

There was a little pause after I'd finished. Then she said: "And did you think all that out by yourself?"

Even after what had happened, I felt disinclined to take responsibility. "No," I said, "my friend George Curtis was the chief architect."

"But you believe it?"

"I—I don't know. I certainly don't want to believe it—but everything seems to point to its being true."

"It's incredible. Doesn't it occur to you that all these things have a perfectly natural explanation? You've strung a lot of trivial little points together and . . . Really, it's monstrous!"

"I'm not sure that a jury will think so."

"A jury! You don't imagine it will come to that? I tell you I can explain everything."

146

"I wish you would."

"Then listen. . . . I decided to call in at Samson that morning simply because after all the shop talk on St. Mary's I thought it might be an amusing change to see what you were doing. Then when you began telling me about the islands I was so interested that I didn't give the launch a thought until it was too late—it was all quite accidental. It's fantastic to think I had any plans. I wasn't paying any particular attention to the conversation in the bar the night before and I certainly didn't realize that that man was going to walk across or that you wouldn't have your own boat to take me back or anything like that. I just wasn't listening. As for deciding to go to Tresco on my own, the fact is that Ronnie had been drunk the night before and I could see he was going to be drunk again and I couldn't face it. I tried to keep the Samson business from him because we'd already had several rows and he was in an unpredictable temper and I didn't want to make matters worse. As for meeting you again on Tresco and going off with you that afternoon . . ."

"Well?"

"I liked you," she said. "Is that so difficult to believe? I liked being with you—very much."

"A few days ago," I said wretchedly, "I'd have been happy to hear you say that. Now I find it hard to accept."

"I'm sorry, because it's true. And you're wrong about everything else as well. When I took your arm and wanted you to leave the ledge there was nothing calculated about it—I simply didn't want either of you to come to harm. And when I made that idiotic blunder and told the rock-climbing story I was thinking of you, too, whatever you may suppose. And all the other things that seem so significant to you—well, they're just an unfortunate combination of circumstances."

"Including the insurance policy?"

"Yes. It may seem surprising to you that a man who hasn't much spare money should take out a huge policy like that, but you didn't know Ronnie. I thought he was crazy, too, and I said so, but he couldn't rest until he'd done it. He really was affected by that man's death in Switzerland, and he said he wouldn't feel like sailing any more, particularly single-handed, unless he knew that I'd be fully provided for if anything happened to him. It wasn't only that, though—he always loved dramatic gestures, and this was a gesture he wanted to make to show how thoughtful and protective he was. He was always doing things like that on my account, and I could never stop him."

"I've been hearing," I said, "a different view about that. I'm actually on my way back now from seeing Ronnie's mother."

Olivia's eyes gave a curious flicker, but whether from anger or fear I couldn't make out. For a moment or two she was silent. Then she said: "That must have been fun for you!"

"It wasn't fun at all, but I learned a good deal."

"I'm sure you did! All about a scheming woman of low social origins who married a man old enough to be her father so that she could live a life of luxury at his expense?"

"That was broadly the picture."

"And you accepted it—from her?"

"Not entirely. But as a background to the facts I already know, some of it seemed pretty telling."

"Naturally it would, because you don't know Ronnie's mother any more than you knew Ronnie. What made you go and see her, anyway? How did you know about her?"

"She wrote to me—she wanted to hear about the accident. If you'd nothing to hide, why didn't you tell her yourself?"

"She'd have burned the letter," said Olivia bitterly. "You don't even begin to understand. She and I have had nothing to do with each other for years. It wasn't my fault—she was as horrible as she could be to me, right from the start. I suppose you were taken in by that gentle manner of hers, that gift she has of saying utterly beastly things in a kindly, understanding way. My God, she's about as gentle as a boa constrictor. I don't know exactly what she said to you, but couldn't you sense how much she hated me? She'd have hated any woman Ronnie had married but she particularly hated me because very soon I realized the harm she was doing to him and tried to free him from her. But it was too late, then—the damage was already done. Surely you could see that she's utterly spoiled and selfish and dominating and that she'd have kept Ronnie emotionally tied to her forever if she'd been able to, and that there's nothing more certain to destroy a man's self-assurance. . . ." She stopped abruptly. "But what's the good of my telling you all this if your mind's made up and your ears are closed to my side of the story?"

"On the contrary," I said, "I'm anxious to hear it, even though I can't promise to believe you."

"What you decide to believe is your affair." There was a little pause, while she seemed to collect her thoughts. Then she said: "Well, to start with, I'm not a gold-digger. When I met Ronnie five years ago I genuinely fell for him. Some women are attracted by older men, and I happened to be one of them. Besides, you never saw him at his best—at that time he was really quite terrific. He'd just come back from Germany and he had a big reputation as a correspondent and he appeared to be full of confidence in himself and he was wonderful company and he was extravagantly in love with me. Altogether I found him irresistible, and I married him. I did more than that —I even gave up my career because he wanted me to."

"Your career?" I echoed. "It's a small point, perhaps— but *was* it such a sacrifice?"

"It was a tremendous sacrifice. I suppose Ronnie's mother has poisoned your mind about that, too? I may not have got very far but at least I'd made a start, at a cost in effort that she couldn't begin to understand. We're not all born with silver spoons in our mouths, and the bottom of the ladder is an awfully long way down."

"I know that," I said. "Please go on."

"Well, as I say, we got married, and it was only after I'd settled down with him that I began to find out what he was really like. I soon discovered that the big, confident, larger-than-life Ronnie I'd married was just a façade—a bold front for the world. There must be thousands of people like that, but Ronnie was an extreme example. His personality had been crushed for so long by that strong-willed, doting mother of his that he'd developed a shocking inferiority complex. All that outward aggressiveness was just a cover for his own uncertainty. He was always trying to prove himself—that was why he ran unnecessary risks as a correspondent, and why he took up hazardous things like sailing and rock climbing. And he had to be different, too—to make an impression on people. That was why he grew that awful beard and insisted on wearing important-looking spectacles that he didn't really need. But actually he was one of the most unhappy men I've ever met. He needed constant reassurance about his work, and his abilities—and about me. Particularly about me. That's why he was so terribly jealous—he could never really believe in the strength of our relationship. That's why he insisted on lavishing things on me—clothes and

150

jewelry and all sorts of luxuries. I didn't want them—it spoils the fun of planning and making when you have perfect things thrust at you all the time. Besides, he couldn't afford them, and I knew that. He even borrowed from his mother in order to buy me things, which was frightful. He liked to show me off, to boast about me to his friends, to build me up into a sort of paragon. It's flattering when it's done nicely but Ronnie did everything to excess. I was his life, practically—it was as though he thought that marrying me was the only really successful thing he'd ever done, which of course wasn't true. But it seemed to become more true as the years went by, because he started to go downhill in his job. The final blow was when he found we couldn't have any children. He was sterile."

"I see."

"It was when he found that out that he started drinking really heavily and then everything went to pieces. He grew more and more extravagant, and more impossible in public, and his temper was frightful, and everything was hopeless. I got him to see a doctor and a psychiatrist but it didn't do any good and I suppose I wasn't much of a help. . . . I *was* sorry for him, terribly sorry, but he wasn't the man I thought I'd married and I simply couldn't pretend I was still in love with him. He knew how I felt, of course, and it was a sort of vicious spiral—one moment he'd be desperately thinking up new ways to please me and the next he'd be practically accusing me of sleeping with his friends when he was out of the house. When he said he was coming down here to get his boat I'd really have preferred to stay behind, but I honestly don't believe he could bear to let me out of his sight."

"And yet he used to go off alone on those sailing expeditions of his," I couldn't help interjecting.

She frowned. "Yes, I know that seems odd, but it was

exceptional. . . . Anyway, we did come down together, and then almost at once that tax story broke. The other reporters arrived and of course Ronnie had to put on his great-man act and he started drinking again and—well, I just couldn't bear it. We had one or two scenes and I told him I didn't think I could go on any longer and I suppose it was that that made him so wildly suspicious when I went off on my own. . . . For me, though, getting away by myself and then meeting you on those lovely islands was like starting life all over again. I felt like a different person, and I suppose I behaved like one. . . . And that's *my* story."

For a moment or two I sat half hypnotized. With her suddenly flushed cheeks and her flashing indignant eyes she looked so lovely and seemed so utterly convincing that I was completely disarmed. I wanted to believe her more than anything in the world. I even had an insane impulse to ask her to marry me the moment we got ashore, because if she did that it would seem to show that Ronnie was really dead and that she was telling the truth! Then I remembered the facts, the cold array of facts, that no amount of artless sincerity could dispose of.

"Leaving aside everything else," I said, "what you tell me doesn't explain the most important thing of all—what happened to Ronnie. He couldn't just have slipped back into the water off that slab, as you suggest, because if he had his body would unquestionably have been found."

She considered that for quite a while. At last she said: "I suppose it is just possible he climbed out and went off somewhere on his own without telling anyone. He'd been very upset, and he was an incalculable person."

"Do you really think that's likely?"

"Frankly, I don't think so. I think he's dead, and that

in time his body will be found. Perhaps it's got wedged in some deep crack in the rocks."

I shook my head. "Every inch of the coast has been examined. It's quite definitely not there."

"The searchers might have missed it—you know how broken up the cliffs are. What about the caves? Has anyone looked in the place we were going to that day—Piper's Hole?"

"It's miles above the water line."

"If he climbed out, he might have gone in there and collapsed."

"People have been in there since."

"What about the other cave?"

"Gun Hole? I looked in there myself. There was nothing."

She gazed at me in silence for a moment. Then she said: "Can you be sure? There was that horrible pool, remember, that seemed to run under the rock. How do you know the body wasn't carried under the rock, too?"

"That's the wildest sort of surmise. There's no evidence that the water goes any distance under the rock."

"There's no evidence that it doesn't. Why, the body may be there all the time! Don't you think someone might have tried to find out before you started to make all these accusations?"

"I can't imagine anyone being prepared to make an underwater search of that pool for the sake of a thousand-to-one chance."

"You only think it's a thousand-to-one chance because you've made up your mind that Ronnie is alive—you, and that precious friend of yours. It seems a reasonable chance to me because I think he must be dead and you insist that all other possibilities have been exhausted. And if the blood was found where you say it was, the cave seems to me just the place where the body might get lodged. Still, I suppose it is easier to stick to theory. It would certainly take a lot more courage than I've got to search a place like that."

"It's a question of sanity," I said hotly, "not courage. If the water does run far under that rock, anyone who went in probably wouldn't come out again. . . . Or perhaps you wouldn't mind that? It would be one way of silencing the principal witness against you!"

She gave me a long stare. "I wouldn't want anyone to go in there. All I'm saying is that it hasn't been tried. You know, you've changed so much I hardly recognize you. You say and believe such incredible things. . . ."

"If I've changed," I said, "it's you who've changed me. You and the horrible facts."

There was no time to discuss the matter any further, for the islands had crept up on us unnoticed and the *Scillonian* was already turning into Hugh Town harbor. As the vessel moved in toward the quay I said: "What are you going to do now you're here?"

"See the police, of course, and tell them what happened on the cliff. And you? Perhaps you'd like to come with me? I expect they'd be very interested in your theory."

I looked at her for a long moment, trying desperately to reach the mind behind the composed mask of her face. We'd had our showdown and I now had all the information I could reasonably hope to get, yet I still didn't know where the truth lay. Either she was a subtle, calculating and utterly unscrupulous woman, or I was a man who had let his imagination run riot on the basis of inadequate data. Either Ronnie was lying low somewhere, waiting for the investigation to die down, in which case I certainly ought to go to the police and denounce them both, or he really was dead, in which case my behavior must seem to Olivia completely unbalanced.

"I think I'll wait a bit," I said.

She gave a faint shrug, picked up her bag, and walked slowly off toward the gangway.

15

My main concern now was to reach Samson as quickly as possible and get George's opinion on the new developments. The Randalls were at lunch, but I managed to find another boatman to run me over to the landing beach and twenty minutes later I was approaching the dig. George had spotted the launch and came ambling along the path to meet me, looking very fit and relaxed. I asked him how he'd been getting on and he told me he'd worked that morning until his hands were blistered—though the trench, I noticed, was only a foot or two longer than when I'd left it.

I quickly brought him up to date with the news. He nodded sagely as I recounted the old lady's views about

Olivia, and was most intrigued to hear about the meeting on the boat, and listened with an air of judicial detachment as I told him all that Olivia had had to say in her own defense. When I'd finished he sat quietly for a moment, thinking it over, and then he slowly shook his head.

"Well, she's a cool customer," he said, "but I'm not persuaded."

"I hardly thought you would be. Just tell me one thing, though. If Ronnie is alive, and she's been in touch with him, why has she come back to Scilly? What would be the point?"

"Surely that's obvious, old boy. Directly they saw Miss Dewey's story in the *Record* they'd realize that people might suspect there'd been a fight. They couldn't afford to let that idea take root, because of the clause about it in the policy, so Olivia was sent back here to reinforce your account of what happened. Which is exactly what she is doing at this moment."

"Would it help them? I've already stated that Ronnie struck at me. For the purpose of an insurance policy, doesn't a blow constitute a fight?"

"I wouldn't know about that, but in any case they'd hardly throw in their hand after all they've gone through —they'd certainly hope for a favorable interpretation. Anyway, I'm willing to bet that Olivia's return is to do with safeguarding the money rather than with safeguarding you."

"But you can't be sure. The whole trouble with this business is that it's impossible to be sure about anything —and that's even truer now than it was before I went away. There are two parallel sets of evidence and they both seem to me about as good as each other and I don't see how on earth one can choose between them. The case against Olivia seems overwhelming until you see her and talk to her, and then it seems unbelievable."

"That's only because you're susceptible. She's evidently an artist in deception and you fall for her tricks every time."

"You must admit she has a plausible explanation for everything."

"For everything except the disappearance of the body, old boy, which is the crucial thing. I wouldn't call that cave stuff much of an explanation."

I had to agree with him there. "All the same, even that can't be ruled out absolutely. The thing is, not much is known about Gun Hole, because it's so rarely accessible. It might be the one place around here where a body could get lodged in such a position that no one could find it."

"Which is probably why Olivia suggested it. She knew the place, and she knew it would be impossible for anyone to say with certainty whether the body was there or not, or to check up. I should say she's simply trying to account for the one vital, unexplained fact in a way that can't be disproved."

"And I'd have thought it couldn't be all that important to them any longer. Even if they'd planned an insurance swindle in the first place, the discovery of the blood must have just about wrecked their chances. I can't believe they'd dare to put in a claim with all sorts of unpleasant suspicions flying around."

"I wouldn't bank on that. It would look pretty strange if they didn't—and they may think suspicion will die down if they don't weaken. For that matter, perhaps Olivia has already put in a claim, or at least notified the insurance company. If so, she'd have no choice but to go on with it. You don't happen to know, I suppose?"

"No, I didn't ask her that."

"Well, it's something the police could easily find out. In any case, if Ronnie has changed his appearance and got to the mainland under an assumed name they're so deeply committed that they've got to keep up the pretense that he's dead, policy or no policy. Don't forget you can be jailed for conspiracy even though it's not successful, and they could hardly find an innocent explanation of his secret departure. I'd go so far as to say that their hope of continued freedom largely depends on the inaccessibility of Gun Hole. Once that place ceases to be a question mark, the case against them is completed."

"Or else exploded," I said. "You know, I think I shall go and take another look at the cave. Tomorrow's the first of the spring tides and I might manage to get inside again if I pick my time carefully. If the pool turns out not to go far under the rock, I may be able to clear the thing up one way or the other in quite a short time."

George shrugged. "Personally, I'd hardly have thought it was worth the effort—it's going to be pretty difficult to prove a negative. It would be much simpler to go to the police. After all, you don't have to commit yourself—all you need do is outline a *prima facie* case and as I said before they'll soon discover if Ronnie is alive."

"Suppose he's not—suppose in the end it's proved that he really is dead?"

"I don't see that much harm will have been done."

"It'll be the end for me as far as Olivia's concerned."

"You mean you seriously want that to go on?"

"I'm crazy about her, George—far worse than ever I was. If I can get at the truth without finally wrecking things between us I intend to. Of course, the damage may already be done, after all my snooping and accusing, but I'm still hoping. Honestly, I feel quite desperate—I don't think there's anything I wouldn't do to prove her innocence and straighten things out with her."

George looked at me derisively. "You're an obstinate cuss. You've met dozens of attractive women in the ten years I've known you, and passed them all up, and now you have to fall for a female criminal!"

"If you saw her," I said, "I think you'd understand. It sounds trite, I know, but to me she's quite different from all other women."

"I'd say that was something we ought to be thankful for! Still, I must admit I'm curious. Do you want me to come with you to the cave tomorrow?"

"I don't think so—it's not really your line of country, and I'll be better alone."

"Then I suggest I go over to St. Mary's and try to have a talk with her while you're on Tresco."

"That's all right with me," I said, "provided you make it clear that you're speaking only for yourself."

He grinned. "I'll tell her that your faith in her is unshaken."

"Just leave me out of it," I told him. "That's all I ask."

After that we dropped the subject and I forced myself to concentrate on the dig. Our work there was definitely not going as we'd hoped. Although the trench had been carried beyond the limits that I'd originally marked out we'd still found almost nothing of significance and the time seemed to have come to strike out in a fresh direction. After a short argument we decided to drive a new trench at right angles to the old one and more or less parallel to the shore. George, still murmuring of blisters, assigned himself the job of staking out the ground with pegs and line and afterward of drawing the sand clear of the parapet while I did the heavy digging. I was glad enough of the hard work, for it had anesthetic qualities and helped to keep my thoughts off Olivia. The excavation progressed rapidly. No one disturbed us during the afternoon, though at sea the launches were active. I caught a glimpse of *Tern,* apparently on her way to St. Martin's, and shortly after five *Seagull* came chugging past us on the regular homeward run. The tide was high enough for Jim to bring her close inshore and I saw him pointing out some object on South Hill to one of his passengers. He waved to us as the boat slipped by scarcely a stone's throw away, and shouted something about the new trench which I couldn't quite catch. No doubt it was one of his pleasantries, for it was followed by general laughter.

We turned in early that night, comfortably tired after our labors, and for a few hours I enjoyed a deep and untroubled sleep. Then, just before three o'clock, something woke me with a terrific start. I had a feeling that I'd heard some loud noise not far away, though I wasn't certain. George was fast asleep—obviously he hadn't stirred. For a while I lay quietly in the tent, waiting to see if the noise would be repeated, but all I could hear was the murmur of the waves breaking on the beach. My ears had evidently deceived me. It was rather annoying, because I was now very wide awake and likely to remain so.

The moment of alarm had left me thirsty and presently I went outside the tent to get some water. Just as I was raising the mug to my lips a fresh sound reached me—a sound like the crackling of dry vegetation. It seemed to come from the vicinity of the stile, about halfway between the tent and the dig. If it hadn't been for the much louder noise that had wakened me, I'd have supposed that some small animal was moving about in the undergrowth. As it was, I felt I'd like to know more.

I moved quietly into the open and stopped to listen

161

again. The night was fine and clear, with a starry sky, but it wasn't possible to see much of the landscape. I took a couple of steps in the direction of the stile—and gave an involuntary grunt of pain as my bare foot came down firmly on a young gorse plant. My discomfiture seemed to be the signal for fresh movement, for there was more crackling in the undergrowth ahead. I advanced another pace or so, and the noise stopped. It was like an eerie game of "Grandmother's Footsteps" and I felt my skin prickle. There was no doubt that something or somebody was retreating toward the stile.

I couldn't bear the tension, and called out sharply, "Anyone there?" For a full minute there was silence. Then, very faintly, I caught the sound again, the sound of a stealthy withdrawal.

I returned to the tent and quickly slipped on trousers and sweater and shoes. My movements aroused George, and he half turned over toward me. "Wassermatter?" he muttered.

"I think there's someone prowling about outside."

He raised himself sleepily on one elbow. "Can't be, old boy. Must have been dreaming."

"I don't think so. Something wakened me—a hell of a row . . . Listen!" Very faintly, through the window aperture of the ruined cottage that sheltered us, the distinctive sound came again. "Hear it? I'm going to have a look round."

He sat up, grumbling. "Hold on a minute, then. Now I'm awake I suppose I may as well come too."

I waited impatiently while he pulled on his clothes and then led the way out into the darkness. I had a torch now, but I kept it switched off and more or less felt my way down the overgrown path, with George close at my heels.

We stopped by the stile and listened again. I didn't believe that if there was anyone about he could have got very far, for every step on the dry vegetation was clearly audible and we'd heard only very cautious movements. But we certainly seemed to be alone now. After a while George said, "There's no one here—you're imagining things. Let's go back and make a cup of tea."

I was almost persuaded. I probed the undergrowth around us with the torch beam but there was no sign of any lurking figure. I was just turning away when George suddenly cried, "I say, look at that!" He was pointing to the stile. I turned the light full on it and saw that the second rung from the top had snapped in the middle. Most of the wood was rotten, but where it had splintered off at the sides there were bits that shone white. The break was a new one. The noise I had heard was the crack of the stile as it broke under the weight of a man!

At once our voices became conspiratorial. "He may be lying low on the other side of the wall," I whispered. "Let's cross."

With infinite care we negotiated the stile and gazed down the slope of heather and bracken toward the dig. It was going to be difficult, I could see, to spot a man in all that undergrowth as long as he kept still. The thing was, could he afford to keep still? If he did, he'd be the loser in the long run, because when daylight came we should find him.

We sat down under the wall, where our silhouettes wouldn't show against the stars, and waited in silence. I felt thankful that George was with me for my nerves were already badly stretched and the thought of an intruder lurking close at hand wasn't very pleasant. Whoever he was, and whatever he was doing there, his presence seemed pretty sinister in that lonely place at night.

We waited for quite a time, but nothing happened,

and presently I decided to try a feint. I explained the plan to George in a whisper and than said in a normal voice—"You're right, George—I must have dreamed it. Let's get back and make that tea." We scrambled to our feet and climbed the stile and then climbed back silently on the same side and stood against the wall, hardly daring to breathe. It was a child's trick, but it worked. Almost at once, something stirred in the bracken only a few yards ahead of us. We moved quickly toward the sound and when I thought we'd about reached the spot I switched on the torch.

Instantly, almost from under our feet, a figure sprang up from the ground and bounded away down the hill. The move was so sudden that, even though we'd been half expecting it, it was unnerving. George let out a cry and in my excitement I nearly dropped the torch. Before I could direct the beam on him the man was away in the darkness.

"After him!" I yelled. We charged down the rough slope at a breakneck pace and crossed the waist hard on the man's heels. He was going all out, by the sound of him, and so were we. He plunged recklessly into the thick tangle of briars on the slope of North Hill and as we pounded after him I could feel the rending of cloth and the vicious drag of thorns at my legs. But there was no question of halting now—we were determined to get him if we could. He was weaving and doubling like a hunted animal but we followed in the wake of the noise and slowly gained on him. Then, suddenly, we ran into trouble. It was shocking terrain for a chase in the dark and I had been afraid that something unpleasant would happen to one of us. It happened to George. As we tore through heather and gorse below the peak of North Hill he caught his foot in a root and took a header into the undergrowth. For a second I hesitated—our quarry was now visible against the skyline and I felt sure I could catch him. But I didn't know how badly George was hurt. I pulled up and went quickly back to him. In fact he was only winded, but it was a minute or more before he could continue and by that time our man had disappeared over the hill and silence had fallen again upon the island.

We held a swift consultation about tactics. Whoever the fellow was, there wasn't much doubt that he'd come by boat that night, and now that he'd been discovered his one aim would be to reach the boat and get away. The landing beach was just over the hill, and he'd seemed to be making for it. If so, there was still a chance that we might reach it before he could launch a punt. I set off up the hill again at top speed, with George laboring valiantly behind me, and in a matter of minutes we reached the beach. But our luck was out. The wide stretch of sand was bare and no sound of oars came from the dark, empty sea.

"The trouble is," I said, as we climbed to the cliff path and sat down to rest, "that he could have drawn out his boat pretty well anywhere with the sea as quiet as it is tonight."

We sat listening for a while, but we might have been alone on the island for all the indication he gave. My guess was that once he'd outdistanced us he'd dropped down in the undergrowth somewhere at the top of the hill and let us pass him. In that case he could have retraced his steps and by now he could be at the other end of the island. It was a pretty hopeless prospect. Our only chance, a slim one, seemed to be to make a quick circuit of the shore and hope that we might reach the boat first. As soon as we'd got our breath back we set off along the path toward the waist, scanning the foreshore for the loom of a dinghy's hull. We'd hardly taken a dozen steps before we heard an unmistakable sound ahead—the scrape of a boat's keel being dragged over shingle. The man had thrown all caution aside and was gambling on a quick getaway. We tore along the path, scrambled down the low cliff to the beach, and plunged into a maze of weedy rocks and treacherous pools. In front of us we could still hear the crunch of the boat, but the noise didn't last long. The fellow had too much of a start. By the time we'd reached the water's edge the punt was twenty yards out and its unidentified occupant was rowing rapidly out to sea. A moment later the darkness closed over him.

We returned to the path, angry and frustrated. There was nothing more we could do—by the time we'd launched our own boat there wouldn't be a hope of catching him. I couldn't feel that we'd been very skillful in our hunt, though in the darkness the odds had always been with him. Soaked with sweat and sea water, aching with bruises and savagely scratched, we sat glumly and discussed the incident.

I said: "Do you suppose it might have been Field?"

"What would he hope to find out at night?"

"I don't know, but he's the only person I can think of who might want to spy on us."

George grunted. "That fellow didn't behave like a policeman—rushing off in a panic the way he did. He was up to no good, that's certain."

"Could it have been someone after our stores?"

"It's not very likely—there's nothing worth pinching. A few tins of food, a few tools . . ."

At the mention of tools I got up and flashed the torch round the dig, but nothing had been disturbed.

"Well, have you any ideas . . . ?"

George's face took on the consciously blank look which so often preceded a highly provocative remark.

"Perhaps it was Ronnie!"

I gave a short laugh. "You certainly have a single-track mind."

"I'm quite serious."

"Nonsense! What would he come back for?"

"To silence the witnesses. After all, he has the best of reasons. We happen to have hit on his secret and he must know that it's only a matter of time before we tell Field. No one else knows the truth. With us out of the way, he'd be safe."

I remembered uneasily that I'd half accused Olivia of wanting to get rid of me for the same reason—but *I'd* blurted it out in hot temper and hadn't really meant it. George did.

"He couldn't know about this theory of yours," I protested. "Nobody knew, until I told Olivia on the boat."

"That was at midday. She could have rung him up and told him directly she landed."

"He wouldn't have had time to get here."

"He would if he was somewhere close at hand—somewhere in Cornwall. He could have flown in during the afternoon. He could have taken one of the punts from the quay after dark and rowed himself over. I see nothing impossible in that."

"It strikes me as fantastic. After all, there were two of us. He couldn't have dealt with both of us at the same time. He couldn't have hoped to."

"If the stile hadn't broken," said George, "we should both have been asleep. And he would naturally have had some weapon—probably a couple of blows would have done the trick. . . . Oh, well, let's go back to the tent and find some iodine—my shins are torn to ribbons."

We climbed the slope in a heavy silence. I didn't for a

moment believe that anyone had come to attack us, least of all Ronnie, but it exasperated me that I could think of no plausible alternative. I stalked ahead, using the torch to guide us. As we reached the place where our visitor had been flushed from the undergrowth I stopped and shone the light on it. He'd left a depression in the bracken, but apparently nothing else. I was turning away to the stile when the torch beam picked out something on the other side of the path. There was a glint of metal, and as I directed the light full onto it I caught my breath in horror.

It was an axe!

For a moment we both stared at it without speaking. Then I bent and picked it up. It had a short haft and a small heavy head with a bright cutting edge that felt as though it had been newly sharpened.

"So I was right!" said George, suddenly pale in the torchlight. "That settles it. My God, we're lucky to be alive."

It certainly settled the motive. There could be only one reason why a man would steal up on a tent in the dead of night with a murderous weapon in his hands. It was more like sheer melodrama than anything that had happened yet, but the axe was the proof. And that wasn't all—the same thought, I knew, was in both our minds. It was only a day or two earlier that we'd seen an axe in the cabin of Ronnie's boat!

Well, of course, there was no hope of any more sleep that night. I made some tea, and we doctored our lacerated legs, and at first light we set out to see if our would-be assailant had left any other traces of his visit. I thought that perhaps there might be some clear footprints, but the sandy waist had already been so churned up by our own comings and goings and by visitors that one print was indistinguishable from another. We went again over the route that we had taken during the night chase, as nearly as we could judge it, but we found nothing else of interest. There were one or two marks in the sandy shingle where the man's boat had been drawn out, but they were indistinct and unpromising.

"Perhaps the police will be able to make something of them," said George. "I suggest we pay a call on Ronnie's boat after breakfast, just to make sure that it is his axe, and then get Field on the job without delay."

"We'll certainly look in on *Truant*," I agreed. "One step at a time!"

We wrapped the axe in a cloth in case there should be any fingerprints on the handle besides our own, and put it carefully away in the tent. We had some food, and then we launched the punt and I rowed across to St. Mary's. It was still barely eight o'clock, and we had the little harbor to ourselves. Once more I tied the punt to *Truant* and climbed aboard.

There were no outward signs that anyone had visited her and my hopes rose—if Ronnie's axe was still there, George would have to think again. But one glance through the ventilator told me that he'd been right. The rope and the paint pots and the tools were still there, but the axe had gone.

George took it quite as a matter of course. "Well, that's that," he said. "A clear case! There isn't going to be much left for Field to do."

I sat down on the stern seat and lit a cigarette.

"You know," I said, "we still haven't proved that it was Ronnie who took the axe."

George looked at me in amazement. "My dear chap, of course he took it. The cabin's locked. Who else would have a key?"

"The Randalls must have one, and we don't know who may have had access to it. I'm still not satisfied, George. I admit that all these new developments do seem to strengthen your theory in some ways, but they certainly don't prove it."

"For heaven's sake! Who else but Ronnie could have any reason for wanting to kill us?"

"I don't know the answer to that question. All I do know is that a lot of very strange things have been happening around here for some time, and I'm not sure that we've got to the bottom of them yet. That business last night must have had something to do with the Ronnie affair, I suppose, but I'm far from convinced it was Ronnie on the island. Even if he's alive, which I still can't accept, coming back would have been a fearful gamble for him. However much he'd changed his appearance, it seems most unlikely to me that he'd have dared to show up again in daylight in the very spot he'd left only a few days before. You can't alter your shape and the way you walk and the general impression you give—not with any certainty that you'll get away with it."

"Don't forget he's desperate. He had twenty thousand pounds at stake."

"So you say. But if he'd succeeded in killing us and anyone had got an inkling that he'd been around, he'd have stood to lose more than money. Anyhow, that's not really the point."

"What is?"

"If you're right, and Ronnie was brought over to kill us, then Olivia's an accessory—morally, she's a murderess herself. I've been trying to imagine her standing in a telephone box and calmly urging Ronnie to come over quickly and butcher the pair of us in our sleep with an axe—and

I can't. I can no more believe it of her than I'd believe it of my own mother."

"She didn't have to do that, you know. All I suggested was that she told him we'd hit on the truth. He could have done everything off his own bat."

"If he'd succeeded, she'd have known. And he'd never have attempted it if he hadn't been sure he could rely on her. If you're right, George, they're in it together, up to the neck, and she's a murderess at heart—and that's what I don't believe."

There was a short silence. It was the old familiar deadlock.

"Anyway, I'm against rushing things," I went on after a moment. "I think at the very least we should give ourselves some time to think it over. What I suggest is that we do as we planned yesterday. I'll go and have a look at Gun Hole and you go and talk to Olivia. If I don't find anything, and if you're still in the same mind, and if the Randalls assure us they haven't let *Truant's* key out of their sight—well, perhaps we'll tell Field in the morning."

"It's a pure waste of a day," said George in a tone of exasperation. "And how do we know the fellow won't take another crack at us? He must still be around here somewhere."

"He won't have the same opportunity again. We can sleep at the Ocean tonight, just to be on the safe side."

"He could pick us off separately in his own time. I've only the vaguest idea what he looks like, and if he's changed as much as I think he has, you haven't much either."

"I'll take the risk."

"This is hardly your exclusive affair any more," George said coldly. "Personally I dislike the feeling that there's a chap around who'd like to split my skull. It seems to me to call for action."

"Well, George, I can't insist—you'll have to do as you like. I'm going to Gun Hole. If it was worth doing yesterday it's worth doing today."

"I doubt if it was ever worth doing. Still, I suppose I'll have to let you have your way." He climbed into the dinghy. "All I hope is that you don't have reason to regret it. Just row me ashore, and you can push off straight away. . . . My God, to think I came here for fun!"

16

An hour later I was back at the tent. I equipped myself with a torch and candles, some sandwiches and coffee, and a long bamboo cane that I'd used on occasion for taking rough measurements at the dig. Then I rowed across to New Grimsby. Once ashore on Tresco, I set off slowly along the winding path past Cromwell's Castle. There was no hurry, for the tide wouldn't be low enough for my purpose until after midday.

I was determined to give Olivia's theory every chance, and when I reached the cliff top I tried to put the incident of the axe out of my mind and concentrate on what might have happened to Ronnie. Up to a point, what Olivia had suggested made sense. Just how and when he had sustained his injury would remain a matter of conjecture, but as I saw it he could have hurt himself during, or quite soon after, his fall, but not too severely, and then suffered more damage as a result of his buffeting on the way to the slab; or of course the initial wound could have been received on his way to the slab. In either case he might have lost consciousness there after he'd hauled himself a little way out—the position of the blood was consistent with a body having been only partially out of the water at the time of the bleeding. He might even have died there. If so, the high tide around six o'clock the next morning might well have washed his body back into the sea and in that case it probably would have been carried toward the Hole, as Olivia had said. There was nothing unreasonable about any of that—as a theory.

I sought out a vantage point above the gully that led to the cave and sat studying the movement of the sea. The surface was again remarkably calm for Scilly but this time the tide was still high enough to create a spectacular effect below me. The water, deep sapphire in color except where it was flecked with spume, kept surging into the narrow rock-bound channel like a great battering ram before retreating to strike again. It was rhythmic and relentless, and as the huge mass poured into the opening of the Hole there came from within the cavern, with each fresh forward stroke, a boom that sounded like the thunder of heavy artillery. It was easy to see how the place had come to be called Gun Hole.

I waited with what patience I could muster for the tide to fall. Twelve o'clock came, and I consumed my sandwiches and coffee, and then I filled in half an hour strolling along the cliff. By the time I returned, an appreciable change had taken place in the appearance of the gully. I was on the point of climbing down to the shelf and working my way along so that I could take a closer look at the depth of water near the entrance when I heard a sound above me and saw that someone was coming down over the boulders toward me in a great hurry. It was just like the day of Ronnie's fall over again except that this time the approaching figure wasn't Ronnie—it was Olivia. When she saw me sitting on the rocks she slowed down.

I found it hard to conceal my inward agitation. It was always the same when I saw Olivia—I was thrown at once into an emotional turmoil. Today it was worse than ever—there was so much I wanted to say to her, and so little that would bear saying. That being so, I'd have preferred to do my investigating unobserved. I wondered why she had come, and my greeting was cold.

She was breathing quickly, and her face as she dropped down beside me had an anxious look.

"I've been talking to your friend George Curtis," she said. "He told me you were thinking of going into Gun Hole again, so I came straight over."

"Why?"

"I thought you might be going to do something stupid."

"You were quite right. I'm going to search for a non-existent body!"

"If you're so certain it's nonexistent there's no point in taking silly risks."

"Well, that's a change of tune from yesterday. You were practically hounding me into the cave then."

"I was angry. You don't have to be childish, just because I said it would need courage."

"Oh, I'm not doing it just to impress you, don't think that. You've put up a theory, and I can't rest now until I've proved or disproved it."

"You won't be able to do either," she said, "not safely. That's what I wanted to tell you. I talked to Barney on

175

the way over and he thinks that pool does go under the rock. He says he'd completely forgotten about it until I brought the subject up, but he remembers now that he heard something about it when he was a boy."

"That's interesting. Did he have any views about the likelihood of the body being there?"

She hesitated. "He thinks it could be, but he says nothing would induce him to go in himself."

"He hasn't got my reasons," I said.

"He's got a lot more sense. What on earth's the point of running into danger for a lunatic idea which you'll have to give up in the end anyway?"

"I've got to find out if it's lunatic or not. Your saying so doesn't make it so."

She sat in silence for a moment, watching the battering ram. At the cave entrance it had lost most of its power and the booming had stopped, but the gully was still pretty awe-inspiring. Her face was very tense.

"In any case," I said, "there can be no harm in a little reconnaissance." I got to my feet. "I can probably get down now. You'd better stay here."

I took off my shoes and socks and rolled my trousers above the knees. I stuck the torch and matches and half pound of candles into a side pocket and picked up the bamboo cane and climbed down the boulders to the seaward end of the gully. It took me only a few seconds to work my way along the rock shelf to the cave entrance. There was still a nasty swirl underneath me but the depth of water was less than two feet and I thought I could make it. I climbed down the crack and lowered myself cautiously into the water until my feet touched the bottom. The force of the surge made me stagger, but I clutched the rock wall and began to work my way toward the Hole.

At that moment I heard a cry behind me. I swung round and saw that Olivia was following along the shelf. She'd come to a halt about halfway along and seemed paralyzed.

"Wait!" I called. "Hold on!" I started to wade back toward the crack. Before I could reach it, Olivia had begun to move again. There was a look of desperate intensity on her face and she came with a rush as though she were determined to finish the journey in one swift movement. A moment later she had reached the crack above me. I hadn't time to say anything more or even extend a hand before she had half scrambled, half fallen down the rock face and was picking herself out of the water beside me, drenched to the skin and pale as a ghost.

"You shouldn't have come," I said harshly. "Are you hurt?"

"No, I'm all right."

"You won't be for long. You know you can't bear this place."

"If you're going in, I'm coming too."

"Well, I'm certainly going in."

I turned again toward the cave. As I reached the entrance and advanced into the darkness I set the candles on ledges and boulders until the whole interior of the cavern was brightly lit. There was only an inch or two of water over the floor and the tide was still running out. In a few minutes the ground would be dry. I picked my way carefully over the boulders and flashed my torch onto the surface of the pool. There was already a watershed between it and the sea, and it was quite motionless.

It looked most uninviting. It was about six feet wide, and as I stood on the brink the rock face under which it seemed to disappear was about eight feet away from me. With the tip of the cane I could just reach it. I tested the water, and it was as cold as it looked. The bottom was firm and sandy, and sloped sharply away from me. I stepped in cautiously and began to probe all around with the bamboo. I thought there was just a chance that a body might have got caught under the water and held there, but I could feel nothing except sand and rock. I advanced further until the pool was lapping round my knees, and then thrust the cane as far forward as I could, under the water. There was no resistance. Barney's recollection was right—the pool *did* go under the rock.

I waded out and stood staring down at the opaque surface. There was no sound in the cave except a steady dripping from the roof and Olivia's agitated breathing behind me. I glanced round at her, and her face was ghastly in the candlelight. She looked terribly bedraggled, and she was shivering, and it wasn't hard to guess what a fearful effort in self-control every second that she was staying there was costing her. At any other time I'd have been deeply concerned for her, but now I could think of nothing but the pool and the secret it might hold. I'd *got* to go on. Swimming under the rock, I told myself, wouldn't be nearly as dangerous as it looked. Probably the water didn't go far under. I could go in and probe around and be out again in a matter of seconds. If the body *was* there, I'd find it, and this long nightmare would be over. Whatever happened, the intolerable uncertainty would be at an end, because if it wasn't there it wasn't anywhere. I felt pretty scared, but in an odd way that only helped to drive me on. There was only one reason why I should turn back now, and that was fear, and if I turned back for that I'd despise myself forever. . . .

"I'm going in," I said. "You'd better wish the witness good luck."

She clutched at my arm, and I could feel her whole

body trembling. "Don't—*please* don't. It's so horrible—I can't bear it."

Her restraining hand acted on me like a spur. It flashed through my mind at that moment that she'd followed me to the cliff and right into this cave that she loathed, precisely because she knew that if I went into the pool I *shouldn't* find anything, and that then the game would be up for her and Ronnie. At all costs she'd got to stop me. I shook myself free.

"Here, take the torch and shine it down into the water." I unrolled the turned-up legs of my trousers and peeled off my shirt.

She shone the torch into the inky pool. There was nothing lovely about her face now—it was a mask of terror and revulsion. "Oh, you're mad. . . . You'll be drowned. I can't let you do it." Her voice had suddenly taken on a new note of resolution. "John, listen to me! There's no need for you to search any more. You'll only be risking your life for nothing."

I was checked by the change in her tone. "For nothing?"

"Yes. I'd never have told you, but I can't let you drown. You were right about Ronnie and me. We did work it all out together."

I stood stock still, while the water dripped around us. "You mean he *is* still alive?"

"Yes, he's alive. He's been staying in Penzance all the time. We were going to Ireland after I'd collected the money. Oh, it seemed so easy. . . ."

I could scarcely bear to look at her. "Then it *was* Ronnie who came after us with an axe last night . . . !"

"With an axe . . . ?" she echoed.

I grabbed the torch and shone it full into her face. "Is

179

this true about you and Ronnie, or is it some new trick to get me out of here?"

"It's true," she said. "It's all true." There were tears in her eyes. I couldn't understand why she should be crying. I couldn't understand her at all. Her confession seemed no more convincing now than her denials. The only certain thing was that she didn't want me to go into the pool. Whether she was scared for me or scared for herself was more than I could guess.

"Well, I don't know whether you did it or not," I said, "but now that I'm here I'm damned well going to find out."

I thrust the torch back at her, took a deep breath, and plunged into the pool, cutting off her cry. I swam down to the base of the rock and underneath it, groping around. The space was narrow, with a sandy floor. There was no sign of a body there—no obstruction of any sort. I felt emptiness ahead and swam forward a couple of strokes and as I reached outward and upward I discovered there was no roof. I surfaced cautiously, and found that I could breathe once more.

I could have laughed at the fuss we'd made about the danger. The water-filled siphon was only a few feet long —scarcely an obstacle at all. On the inside, the bottom of the pool shelved up again and I scrambled out onto shingle. The darkness was absolute, but now that I was here I'd obviously got to explore the whole place. If the body *had* been washed under the rock it could easily have been carried up to the head of the cave at high water.

I picked my way over rounded boulders, feeling between them, feeling both walls as high as I could reach. The search didn't take long—the passage narrowed quickly, with what seemed a gentle rise away from the sea. I covered every inch of the ground, right up to the jagged cleft where the cave ended. The body wasn't there.

So Ronnie *was* still alive, and Olivia's confession was true!

At the thought of Olivia, I suddenly realized what I'd done. *She* didn't know there was a way out of the pool on the inside—by now she must be certain that I'd been drowned. I turned and rushed with careless haste back over the boulders. I'd scarcely taken a step when one of the stones rocked under me and I missed my footing and fell heavily. My head hit something so violently that it was filled with a blinding light. Then all sensation left me.

17

I came to with a splitting headache and a feeling of nausea. There was the taste of blood in my mouth, and when I cautiously touched my scalp I found a huge lump above the right ear. My joints were stiff from lying in the damp cold and it was all I could do to struggle into a sitting position.

As I slowly collected my scattered wits I became aware of noise in the cave. The tide was coming in and the battering ram had started up again. I must have been unconscious for quite a while.

I got to my feet with a sudden sense of urgency and tottered down the slope, supporting myself against the rough rock wall. Almost at once my feet splashed into the pool. The water had already advanced many yards up the inner cave—just how far, in the pitch darkness, I had no means of judging. But one thing was instantly clear—for the time being, I was a prisoner. The pool inside was not as turbulent as the gully outside, but the water was driving in under the rock with enormous force and I hadn't a hope of swimming out against it. I should have to wait until the tide was low again, which wouldn't be until the early hours of the morning.

It was a grim prospect. I was already chilled to the bone, and I had no food, no drink, and no light. The thought of Olivia rushing off to report a new drowning wasn't exactly cheering. The recollection of her duplicity was like a leaden weight on my mind. One way and another, I felt pretty sorry for myself.

I bathed my face and moistened my dry lips with a brackish trickle from the roof. Then I tried to restore my circulation by slapping my arms across my chest, but the pain in my head was so acute that I had to give that up. Instead, I began to walk up and down the sandy slope, feeling my way with care among the tumbled debris. I counted about fifteen steps from the water's edge to the head of the cave when I started walking, but in what seemed a matter of minutes the distance was halved. The tide was rising at a tremendous rate. Suddenly, with a shock of panic, I realized that the place might fill completely at high water.

I turned in alarm and scrambled quickly to the end of the passage. The darkness was so intense that there was no chance of my eyes getting used to it—I couldn't even sense my hand outstretched an inch before my face. But I could still feel, and what my exploring fingers discovered was far from reassuring. All the rock that I touched seemed wet. The roof of the cave at the point farthest from the sea was about ten feet high—I could just reach it after I'd climbed the narrow cleft in the granite. The roof was wet, too. I told myself that the moisture could be the result of condensation or splash—but my heart sank.

It seemed just possible that there might be a higher bit of roof somewhere else and I worked my way up one fissure after another in the cave walls in the hope of finding a safe retreat. It was exhausting work in the darkness, and I had no success, but it kept me warm and helped to pass the time. At one point I found a break in the ceiling through which air seemed to be escaping to the world above, but it was a mere crack and offered no way out for me.

By now the din was deafening. Every thrust of the battering ram outside reverberated in the cavern like an explosion. The creeping water had almost covered the sandy floor and soon I was driven back against the rock at the head of the cave. I climbed again into the cleft and the water began to slap and swirl at my feet. There was no phosphorescence, no gleam of foam—only noise.

It was terrifying beyond description. I remember thinking, as the heaving mass began to drag at my legs and I struggled a little nearer to the roof, that these spring tides probably weren't as high as the ones two weeks before and that it must be only the highest tides that actually filled the cave, but I wasn't sure enough to find much consolation in the thought. Presently I ceased to think. Fear entered and possessed me, and I became an animal recoiling instinctively from death, drawing away to the uttermost limit to postpone the end. I lost all sense of time. Under the repeated shock of the battering ram my mind grew numb. Half immersed, my body lost all feeling, too. I was no longer aware of throbbing head and aching limbs. I was scarcely aware of misery. The limits of my consciousness were surging water and a rocky roof.

The tide must have turned some minutes before I realized it. It was only when I found that parts of me which had been covered were now uncovered that the paralysis of mind ended. I had missed death literally by inches and now it was a matter of will—of fighting the cold, of sticking it out, of waiting. Hope gave me strength. As the waters receded from the sand below me I lowered myself stiffly to the ground and began to slap and massage my legs and feet. When there was space enough I started to walk again, up and down, up and down, knowing that at all costs I must keep moving. I thought of the warm air outside, of the wonderful sun that I should see rise again, of the sheer joy of being alive and not dead. That kept me going.

The falling tide marked the passage of time for me now; that, and the slow diminuendo of the noise. When at last the racket stopped I knew the waves had ceased to hammer at the walls outside, though that didn't mean the cave was dry. In any case I should still have to wait for the water level to drop in the gully. I was desperately weak; it would be idiotic to move too soon, to risk a long swim when a few feet should suffice.

Presently the surface of the pool became completely still—the seas were no longer running into the cave. In half an hour, I decided, it should be possible to negotiate the gully. But how to measure half an hour? To leave it too long would be worse than to start too soon. I paced up and down, counting seconds, building them up into minutes. Finally I decided I would give myself five more trips up and down and then I would go.

I was well up in the cave on the last trip when there was a splash in the pool behind me. I thought it must be a crab or a fish but a second later the blackness of the cave was pierced by a shaft of brilliant light. I gave a cry, and the light advanced to meet me.

It was Barney! As he reached me he gripped my arm in fierce, incredulous relief. "God," he said, "I felt sure you were dead. Are you all right?" He flashed the torch over me in anxious scrutiny.

"I think so," I said weakly. Now that help had come I realized how very far from right I was. "I got a bit of a crack on the head. . . ."

"Don't worry, we'll get you out. I brought a rope with me, and there are folks waiting at the other end."

He gave me a hand and I leaned heavily on him as I stumbled back to the pool. I doubted now if I'd ever have had the strength to get back unassisted.

"It was decent of you to come in and look for me, Barney," I said.

"Couldn't just leave you here, could I?" He gave me the waterproof torch to hold and began to tie a bowline under my arms. "I've arranged signals. They'll pull you out gently."

"What about you?"

"I'm all right—I'll be close behind you."

I handed the torch back. As I passed it to him the swinging beam of light focused on the wall of the cave, high up near the roof, and something white caught my eye.

"Barney—look!"

He held the beam steady and we both stared.

"Christ!" he said softly.

Jammed in a horizontal cleft was the body of Ronnie Kendrick. The head was lolling back in space, horrible to see, and across the forehead there was a great gash.

18

I got through the siphon without any difficulty and so did Barney. There was a large and agitated group waiting in the outer cave with hurricane lamps and torches—Jim, and one of the "lads" and several Tresco men and, of course, George and Olivia—and I can still hear the gasp of amazed relief as I emerged from the pool on the end of the rope. Everything was very confused for a few moments, but I remember the parchment yellow of George's thin features as he helped to pull me out, and the look of inexpressible thankfulness on Olivia's face as for a second she took my hand. There wasn't much opportunity for questions or congratulations because the gully was filling up again and we all had to get up the rock pretty quickly.

Someone provided me with a raincoat and sweater when we reached the cliff top and I put them on while Barney broke the news about the body. Olivia gave me one glance —that was all. She looked utterly worn out, and presently she set off across the moor with Jim. George and Barney helped me and the others brought up the rear. The "lad" had been sent ahead to rouse the inn and by the time we got there hot blankets and drinks and food had been prepared. The Randalls soon departed, taking Olivia with them. All she said on leaving was "Good-by!—I'm glad you're safe." I hadn't the strength to do anything but nod. A few minutes later I was assisted up to bed, and this was one occasion when even worry couldn't keep me from sleeping like a log.

The awakening next morning was pretty grim. Apart from a bruised head there wasn't much wrong with me physically, but when I thought about Olivia I felt un-utterably wretched. She'd behaved so well about every-thing, all the way through, and I'd come out of it so badly. George, too, was sunk in gloom. Apparently he'd been enormously impressed by Olivia during their brief encounter, which only made matters worse now. He was deeply and genuinely sorry about his part in the affair, but I was too sore over my own stupidity to respond. It was a good thing, perhaps, that we had plenty to occupy us. Just before noon, Barney and Jim came over with one of the constables and Field and a coastguard and we all went off to Gun Hole with a stretcher. The approach was even more difficult now, for the gully didn't empty as it had done the day before, but the police were determined to recover the body if they could. Barney, having once been inside, didn't seem to mind making the passage again, but Jim and the constable followed more apprehensively. It was touch and go whether they could beat the tide, but they managed it, and half an hour later the remains of Ronnie Kendrick had been brought out on a rope and the party was on its way back to New Grimsby.

It was only then that George and I began seriously to consider the part of the mystery that was still unsolved—the identity and motive of the man with the axe. In a sense, the discovery of Ronnie's body had made things more obscure, not less, for why any other man should have wanted to attack us was something we were as far from explaining as ever. Yet the details of that chase, and the recollection of the axe gleaming in the bracken, were vivid in our minds, and the incident was hardly one we could dismiss as unimportant. The obvious course was to tell the police, but I was reluctant to do that until the inquest on Ronnie was over. It was very much in my mind that I was by no means out of the woods yet—people might still think that I'd fought with Ronnie, and inflicted an injury on him, and then knocked him over the cliff. To announce at this stage that some unknown person had tried to kill me with an axe would inevitably confuse an otherwise simple issue and—since it sounded most unlikely—would probably prejudice a jury against me. This time, George fully agreed.

On the way back to the inn I took Barney aside and told him as tactfully as I could that there was still one little matter I hadn't cleared up but that I couldn't give him the facts for a day or so. In the meantime, would he tell me the position about the key to *Truant's* cabin. He looked surprised, but he replied at once that there was only one key, apart from any that Ronnie might have had, and that it was always kept on a brass hook hidden away under the ship's gunwale. It was a place, I gathered, where no one would be in the least likely to find it unless he knew where to look. I asked him who did know where to look, and after a moment's thought he said he didn't imagine anyone knew except Jim and himself. That made the mystery even more baffling. George and I continued to discuss the affair after the stretcher party had left but we got no nearer a solution. In the meantime, neither of us felt much like sleeping in the tent again, so we arranged to spend another night at the inn.

The inquest was held at Hugh Town on the following afternoon—and from the beginning things went well. The medical evidence, in particular, was most helpful. It turned out that Ronnie's injury was not only consistent with his having come into violent contact with a rock while he was in the water, but the fact that a small piece of seaweed had been extracted from the wound clearly proved that that was how it had been caused. That still left open the possibility that I might be held responsible for knocking him over the cliff, and although I'd always believed that a true story frankly told should carry conviction my anxiety hadn't abated. But I'd reckoned without Olivia—she was superb. She looked frightfully tired, of course, for she'd been under constant strain for a couple of days and only that morning she'd been required to make a formal identification of Ronnie's body, which must have been horrible for her, but she gave her evidence in a clear, confident tone and I marveled that I could ever have mistrusted her. The coroner asked her a question or two about the rock-climbing story and she said that that had been entirely her fault and explained why she had told it and said she was sorry with such quiet dignity that the court seemed very favorably impressed. My turn came next, and I simply confirmed her account. No one made any unpleasant suggestions and the police offered no evidence. Field sat placidly in the back of the courtroom, an interested but inactive spectator. In the end without retiring the jury brought in a verdict of accidental death and the coroner expressed sympathy with the widow. The proceedings couldn't have been more considerate.

I had hoped to catch Olivia after the inquest and make at least an attempt at an apology, but as the court broke up Field buttonholed me. Regrets seemed to be the order of the day.

"I just wanted to say, Mr. Lavery, that I hope that conversation of ours on Samson didn't cost you too much sleep."

"I've missed so much sleep lately," I said, "that I've rather lost count of the reasons."

He nodded understandingly. "I was fairly sure from the beginning that you were telling the truth and when I talked to Mrs. Kendrick I hadn't a doubt about it, but you'll understand that we had to clear up that business of the blood and the disappearance of the body."

"I appreciate that."

He still lingered. "It just shows," he said, "how careful one has to be about circumstantial evidence."

"It does," I said grimly.

"And about telling the truth," he added, with a touch of his old complacency. "If you should ever get into a predicament like that again, Mr. Lavery, which isn't very likely, I would strongly advise you to be perfectly frank from the start. It always pays in the end." He gave me a smile which I'm sure was meant to be friendly and nodded good-by. It would have given me pleasure at that moment to jolt him out of his self-satisfaction by telling him of the hatchet man, but I could think only of Olivia and disengaged myself quickly.

I got caught up with the reporters, including a congratulatory Miss Dewey, outside the building, and by the time I'd freed myself from them Olivia had disappeared and my opportunity had gone. I saw her briefly at the funeral later that afternoon but she showed no inclination to talk then and it was no time to thrust myself upon her. Soon afterward I heard that she'd left for London. When George and I went along to the police station to see Field, we learned that he'd left, too. One way and another, we'd made a botch of our interviews.

There was nothing left but to tell our story to the constable. He listened with interest and no little surprise, which was understandable. In the broad light of day and in the quiet security of Hugh Town, our account of an unidentified assailant with an axe must have sounded quite incredible, particularly as we both declared that as far as we knew we hadn't an enemy in the world.

"Well, it beats me," he said, after he'd put forward various unlikely explanations and had them all turned down. "You don't suppose it was someone having a bit of a game with you?—sort of practical joke?"

"We do not," said George. "This chap meant business."

"If he did, sir, he must have been balmy, that's all I can say. Someone around off his chump." The constable closed his notebook. "Anyway, I've got all the particulars and tomorrow we'll go over to Samson and collect the axe and have a look at those footprints. And I'll make a report, of course. Not much more we can do for the moment."

We agreed, and left it at that.

I was in a pretty beaten frame of mind as we turned in to the Ocean bar. Any further discussion of the Ronnie affair would have been completely barren, yet I had no desire to talk about anything else. It was too late to visit the dig, and in any case I didn't feel I could recapture my early interest. If we'd unearthed St. Samson's mummy

I'd scarcely have noticed. We ordered a couple of whiskies and sipped them broodingly.

Presently George said: "Look, old boy, we can't go on like this. What are you going to do about Olivia?"

"What can I do?" I said gloomily. "She's made her attitude plain—she obviously doesn't want to have anything more to do with me, and I don't blame her."

"I don't think you can be certain of that. It's natural she should feel fed up at the moment, but it may not last."

I smiled a little sourly. "You know, George, I don't think I've much faith in your views about women."

"That's natural, too. All the same, I think you should make an effort."

"What do you suggest?"

"You could grovel. I believe it's often effective."

"I doubt if it would be in this case. As I see it, it isn't just a question of wounded pride. The truth is, I've destroyed any basis for a relationship between us. Once you've thought a woman capable of a mean, sordid crime, and let her see it, there's nothing to build on—and that's what I did in the cave."

"Well, she confessed, didn't she?—you're not a mind reader. Besides, you went under that rock afterward, which showed as plainly as anything could that you didn't really believe it. I'd say that wipes the slate."

I shook my head. "The fact that I could have doubted her to the extent I did would always be a barrier. . . . I think I've had it."

"And I think you're being defeatist. Don't be an ass about this, John—if you don't do anything about her now you'll always regret it, and so shall I, because I'll feel responsible. She must care for you a hell of a lot or she wouldn't have gone to such lengths to keep you from going into the pool. And you care for her. Surely that's a basis? I'd say that all that's needed is for someone to make a move—and it's obviously got to be you."

I was still thinking that over when Barney came in and joined us. He was looking a bit tired round the eyes and gratefully accepted a large whisky from George. I guessed he was feeling the strain of his arduous efforts over the Ronnie affair and it seemed I was right for after about ten minutes he gave a weary sigh and said he thought he'd be pushing along. "An early supper and bed won't come amiss," he said.

"I doubt if we'll be late ourselves," I told him.

"Are you going back to Samson tonight?"

"No, we're staying here. We're in the mood for soft beds."

He smiled, and said he'd be seeing us.

We had a leisurely dinner and a few more drinks, and I began to feel slightly more human. I suggested we should take a short stroll before we turned in and as George was agreeable we walked through the town and up onto the golf links. The night was starlit, with a luminous sea and a clear air. Away to the north, the humped outline of our island was just visible.

"Wish you were there?" said George.

"Not me! I shan't quickly forget that night."

"If only we could get to the bottom of the business! I don't want to spend the rest of my life looking over my shoulder."

We stood in silence for a while, gazing out over the harbor. I was about to suggest that we should make our way back when George suddenly clutched my arm. "I say, isn't that a light?"

"Where?"

"On Samson?"

At first I couldn't see anything, but after a moment my

eyes became aware of a faint glow between the two hills. It disappeared almost at once, but as we continued to watch we saw it again. It was a pool rather than a point of light.

"You're right," I said. "There's someone there."

"Then it must be the same chap—trying to finish the job!"

"What, with a light?"

"Who else could it be at this hour?"

I felt a tingle of excitement. By now all desire for a cozy bed had left me. "Let's go and find out," I said. "This may be our chance."

"I'm game, old boy."

We walked quickly back through Hugh Town and down to the deserted quay. Our punt was tied up with the rest of the Randalls' boats and took a bit of extricating. As I worked among them I suddenly became aware that the most conspicuous one of the lot was missing.

"That's odd," I said. "I don't see Barney's punt."

"He must have left it further along."

"He doesn't usually. . . . Half a minute, I'll go and look." I climbed the stone steps and walked rapidly along the whole length of the quay. There was no doubt about it—the white punt wasn't there. It looked very much as though it was Barney who'd gone to Samson!

"And he was talking of turning in early!" said George. "I say, do you think we've been taking him too much for granted? After all, he did have access to that cabin. . . ."

I was horrified. "Barney would never have come after us with an axe, I'm sure of that. Good God, he risked his life on my account only a couple of days ago. Besides, what possible reason could he have?"

"What reason has he for being on Samson now? John, there's something very funny going on. I'm wondering if that axe business might have been an attempt to scare us off the island."

"If so," I said, "it certainly succeeded!"

"Exactly. And this is the first night that we're known not to be sleeping there—and it's Barney who knows. Come on, let's get cracking."

19

It was a smooth trip, but a long one. The spring ebb was well advanced, and in order to approach the landing beach it was necessary to keep close to the Tresco shore and then make a wide sweep round the dried-out flats. I concentrated on the rowing while George gave me directions, interspersed with a running commentary on the appearance and disappearance of the Samson light. It seemed, he said, to be coming from the waist.

We drew in to the beach at about half past eleven and hauled out the boat. I tied the painter to a rock and then led the way quickly up the slope. We hadn't gone more than a dozen yards before a white object gleamed out of the darkness. It was Barney's punt.

Feeling pretty tense, we set off along the cliff path toward the waist. By now I knew its twists and turns almost by heart and we were able to make our way without too much noise. As soon as we'd cleared the last shoulder of hill and had an uninterrupted view of the dig we dropped down into the undergrowth to study the position. All I could see at first was a patch of diffused light coming up from the ground, but after a while I was able to make out the figure of a man moving to and fro across it. Then I caught the low rumble of voices. There seemed to be two of them there.

We strained our eyes and ears. There was a lot of activity going on, but it was impossible to know exactly what was happening. Short of waiting for daylight, the only way to find out was to go and look, and that needed quite an effort of will. Whatever these two were up to, there wasn't much doubt it was illicit, so we could hardly expect a friendly welcome. But if one of them was Barney, I couldn't believe we should come to any serious harm. George was less sure, but he was prepared to take a chance, and a moment later we got boldly up from the bracken and strode across the remaining hundred yards to the trench.

We were spotted almost as we moved. I heard one of the men say, "My God, there's someone coming!" and I recognized the voice. It was Jim Randall's. Then we were up to them. There was a hurricane lamp in a hollow scooped out at their feet, and by its light I saw the other man's face. It wasn't Barney. To my utter astonishment, it was my old bird-watching acquaintance, Tony Sutton.

"Well, hello!" I said, after I'd recovered from the shock. "Mind if we join the party?"

There was a moment of highly uncomfortable silence. I could only guess what was passing through Sutton's mind, but he had a shovel in his hands and a dangerous look in his eye and I thought for a second he was going to get nasty. But he made no move. He just stared at us. Then his face broke into a rather sickly grin and he put the shovel down and lit a cigarette.

"Looks as though we've been caught in the act, Jim," he said.

The tension eased, and George and I had a chance to take in the quite remarkable scene at our feet. Our T-shaped trench was just as we'd left it, but a couple of yards beyond the point where we'd last been working, another trench had been opened up at right angles, turning the whole excavation into a rough H. The new trench was shallower than ours, and not so wide, but it was a good seven or eight yards long. The two of them must have been hard at it ever since their arrival.

Beside the trench, thrown higgledy-piggledy on the loose earth, were about twenty wooden kegs.

I caught Jim's eye. "So there really *was* some buried treasure!" I said. I lifted one of the kegs. It weighed fifty or sixty pounds, and it was full of liquid. "What is it?"

"Brandy," said Jim. His expression was an odd mixture of defiance and chagrin.

"How did it get here?"

He hesitated.

"Come on," I said, "let's have the whole story. It's bound to come out now so you might just as well be frank."

He glanced at his companion, who gave a shrug of resignation. "I guess he's right, Jim."

"Well," said Jim awkwardly, "the stuff's been here since autumn, as a matter of fact. You see—well, I was rowing back from Bryher one night—at least, it was about two o'clock in the morning—and I happened to hear a noise coming from the beach here and I came in close and found a couple of men digging. So I landed to find out who they were and what they were doing and one of them was Sutton here and the other was Kendrick. . . ."

"Kendrick!" At last I began to see daylight—not much, but a gleam.

"That's right. They'd brought the kegs over from his boat and they were burying them and . . ."

Sutton cut in. "Look, why don't we all sit down and relax? As you say, you'll obviously want the whole story now and you might just as well have it in the proper order."

I didn't quite know what his game was, but he'd evidently decided to be affable and from our point of view the more he talked the better. I had a feeling he'd be less loquacious later on. George found a seat on the upturned wheelbarrow and I squatted down on one of the kegs.

"Right," I said, "go ahead."

Sutton drew on his cigarette and paused a moment. Then he said: "Well, old boy, it's a perfectly ordinary smuggling story. Last spring I happened to meet Ronnie Kendrick on one of his assignments, and we got talking over a few drinks. He told me he was hard up and wished he could raise a bit of extra dough and he said he knew how he could do it if he could get some help. It turned out he owned a boat and had some useful contacts and he was quite prepared to go into the smuggling racket in a modest way if he could get someone to help him sail *Truant*. I'd done a bit of sailing, so to cut a long story short I said I'd go with him, and soon after . . ."

He broke off, and gave a boyish smile. "Perhaps we'd better draw a veil over the early part of last summer, though—there's no point in incriminating myself unnecessarily, so we'll move along to September. Ronnie had fixed up a long weekend for himself, and about the middle of the month we sailed his hooker over to France and picked up these kegs from a bloke he knew. Everything went fine until we were nearly home, and then the weather changed and we got caught out in an easterly gale. I guess you know about that?"

"I heard Ronnie talking about it in the pub," I said. "He gave the impression that he was on his own when it happened."

"Well, he wasn't—luckily for him. We took a hell of a beating—smuggling isn't money for jam, believe me. The rudder was smashed and the mizzenmast went overboard and the engine packed up and we drifted down channel out of control. I felt certain we'd had it. Then the storm let up and we rigged a jury rudder and the next evening we crept in here. We hit a submerged rock on the way through the islands, just for good measure, but we plugged the leak and in the end we managed to bring up safely off Cromwell's Castle."

"It's a good story," I said. "Go on."

"The thing was, what were we going to do with this stuff—twenty kegs of the best? *Truant* was in a shocking mess—before we could put to sea again she'd have to be repaired, which might take months, and we obviously couldn't leave the brandy aboard. In the end we decided to row the stuff ashore and bury it and try to collect it later on. Ronnie suggested Samson because nobody much comes here in the winter and he knew a good place to dig. There was a bit of a problem about tools, but we had a stroke of luck there—Ronnie spotted a workman's hut near the Castle and we broke in and borrowed a shovel and pick, just for the night. We had to make several journeys with the kegs but we got them all ashore at last and everything seemed to be going according to plan—and then suddenly Jim showed up. That took us completely by surprise."

"So I can imagine! I suppose you offered him a cut?"

"It seemed the obvious thing to do."

I looked at Jim. "And you took it?"

"Well, what's a bit of smuggling?" he said with a slightly shamefaced grin. "It's not a crime, is it?—not my idea of one, anyway. Besides, there wasn't much else I *could* do but go in with them. . . ."

"You mean they threatened you?"

He looked quite shocked. "You don't think I'd have stood for that! No, the fact is—well, I'd been meeting a girl on Bryher that night, a visitor, and I knew Barney would raise hell if he found out. And if I'd said anything about what I'd seen I'd have had to explain what I was doing out with a punt at that time of night."

"Very awkward," I agreed.

"So as I'd got to keep my mouth shut anyway, I didn't see why I shouldn't make a bit out of it. I helped them with the kegs, and next day Kendrick fixed up for me to do the repairs on *Truant* and I promised him I'd keep an eye on the place where the stuff was buried."

I gazed round the desolate expanse of sand. "As a matter of interest, how did you know where you'd hidden it?"

"There were two big stones," he said, "in line with the trench."

"Ah, yes." I remembered noticing two stones when I'd been choosing our own site, but of course I hadn't attached any importance to them. "So then what happened, Jim?"

"Well, as soon as Barney and I had fitted out our own boats I started the repairs on *Truant* and I got her finished about three weeks ago. I was going to let Kendrick know she was ready and that he could fetch her any time he liked and then Barney told me you and Mr. Curtis were

202

coming down to dig on Samson. So I wrote off to Kendrick right away and said he'd better look sharp if he didn't want to risk having the stuff dug up."

"And that's what started it all?"

"That's what started it," said Sutton. "Ronnie rang me up and we came straight down here."

"Why didn't you get the stuff away before I arrived?"

"We couldn't make it. Ronnie got caught up in that tax story and he said he wasn't going to jeopardize what was left of his job for a share in a few hundred quid, and I didn't feel I could sail *Truant* away single-handed, and of course Jim was busy. So I just stuck around, giving you that bird-watching line and waiting for Ronnie to be free. Then, of course, the poor devil had that accident, and frankly I didn't see how I'd ever get the stuff away."

"Well, you've dug it up now. What were you going to do with it tonight?"

"Only move it out of your way—find a safer place."

"We'd been watching you," Jim explained, not without relish, "all the time you were digging. There didn't seem much danger you'd find the kegs, not at first, but when I came by in *Seagull* a couple of days ago I saw you'd started a new trench and all of a sudden you were practically up to them. I told Sutton, but there wasn't anything we could do about it as long as you were here. Then, tonight, Barney happened to mention that you were going to stay in Hugh Town so I rushed out and collected Sutton and we came straight here."

"Well, that explains a lot," I said. "I'm still puzzled about one thing, though, Sutton. If you arrived here with Kendrick last September, surely you must have been seen together? How did he manage to give the impression that he sailed in alone?—and how have you got away with your pretense of not knowing him, these last two weeks?"

Sutton smiled. "That's easy. After we'd buried the stuff that night I got Jim to put me ashore on St. Mary's and I caught the *Scillonian* first thing in the morning. I had a few things to attend to. . . ."

"Like telling the people who were waiting for the kegs what had happened?" said George.

"Something like that."

"I thought you said it was Ronnie who had the contacts?" George pressed him.

"Someone had to stay and look after the boat," said Sutton smoothly, "and Ronnie was the obvious chap for that. So I did the other chores. Anyway, that's the answer to your question, Lavery. No one around here ever saw Ronnie and me together—except Jim. And that, I think, is the whole story. . . . The question now is, what are you two going to do about it? I don't know whether you've strong views about smuggling, but the fact is if you give us away young Jim here will be in a packet of trouble, and it won't be exactly pleasant for Ronnie's widow, and I'll probably get six months. Any chance of your giving us a break?"

I realized now why he'd been so disarmingly friendly and frank. I said: "Suppose we did—what about the stuff?"

"If Jim's agreeable, I suggest we simply bung it back and forget about it."

"H'm! Well, we can discuss that when we've *really* had the whole story."

He looked puzzled. So did Jim. "I don't know what else I can tell you," he said. "I've answered all your questions to the best of my ability. . . ."

"What were you doing here last Thursday night?"

"Last Thursday night?" he echoed. Slowly he shook his head. "There must be some mistake. We weren't here then, were we, Jim?"

"Jim wasn't, but you were. We chased you round the island—remember?"

"Sorry, old boy, I don't know what you're talking about."

I looked at Jim. "Did you know he was here on Thursday night?"

"No," he said.

"Well, you might like to hear what you've got yourself into." I told him about the noise in the night, the stile, the chase, and our discovery of Ronnie's axe in the bracken. "And Sutton," I concluded, "is the only person except Barney and yourself who would have known where to find the key of *Truant's* cabin."

Sutton gave a short laugh. "You're on the wrong track, Lavery. I don't know whether this story of yours is true or not, but it certainly wasn't me. I was in bed."

I got off the keg. "Jim," I said, "hold the lamp up a moment. I want you to have a look at your friend's legs."

"Oh, no, you don't," said Sutton, scrambling to his feet. "And don't try to start a roughhouse, Lavery, or you'll get more than you bargained for. We're two against two, don't forget."

Jim looked from Sutton to me and back again. Then he said: "If you've been up to any funny business, Sutton, we're three against one. Let's have a look at your legs."

"Why, you rat . . . !"

Jim grabbed him and dropped him to the ground as though he'd been a child. I rolled his trousers above the knees and George held the lamp close. I hadn't any doubt what we'd find, and I was right. Both legs were lacerated from thigh to ankle.

"All right, Jim," I said, "you can let him go."

"I don't know what you think you've proved," Sutton muttered. "I got that taking a short cut on Tresco."

"He got it tearing through the brambles on North Hill," I said. "Look at *my* legs."

Jim looked. Then he turned to Sutton. "What was the idea?"

"Our impression," said George, "was that he'd come here to kill us."

"I tell you," said Sutton again, "I wasn't here."

"You're wasting your breath," I said. "You seem to forget you left footmarks all over the island. *And* finger-prints on the axe handle. You won't have a hope when the police get to work."

It was a bluff, but it came off. He was silent for a full minute. Then he gave a little grunt of disgust and said, "Okay, Lavery, you win. I *was* here."

"Why did you deny it?"

"Because I didn't want an attempted murder charge pinned on me, of course—I could see you'd got the wrong idea about the axe. You really are making a mistake, you know—I had no intention whatever of doing you any harm. Use your brains, man!—how do you think it would have helped me?"

"Then what did you come for?"

"Just to look around—sort of reconnaissance. I wanted to have a look at your new trench, and I wanted to make quite sure we knew exactly where the kegs were. I thought perhaps I'd dig one of them up, just to make sure. I'd have told Jim the next day, but after that chase and all the excitement I thought perhaps I'd better keep quiet about it."

"What were you doing near the tent?" asked George.

"I merely wanted to make certain you weren't likely to disturb me."

"Make certain with an axe?"

"No, you fool, I . . ." He broke off, hesitating. "I

206

brought the axe along because I remembered there were some roots in the sand. Sort of extra tool, that's all."

George gave a contemptuous snort. The fellow's explanation was derisory—we all knew that. A spade would have cut any root he was likely to find—he certainly wouldn't have gone to the trouble of calling in at *Truant* for an axe, just for that. Yet I could see his point about us —there *wasn't* any good reason why he should have wanted to attack us. So why had he brought the axe? What *could* one do with an axe on Samson? What was there to use it on?

I gazed over the mutilated ground, the scattered barrels—and suddenly I had an idea.

"I suppose it wasn't anything to do with the kegs, was it?"

"Nothing at all. I've told you what it was for."

I went over to the pile of barrels and lifted one of them, and then another. Soon George joined me—he'd got the idea, too. Sutton sat motionless, watching us, and Jim watched him.

Almost at once we found what we were looking for. I picked up a keg that stood a little apart from the others, and it felt different. It was lighter.

"George," I said, "would you mind fetching the axe?"

He strode off with unaccustomed alacrity, and in less than five minutes he was back. I took the axe and began to hack away at the keg. It was well made and tough, but the tool hadn't been freshly sharpened for nothing and after half a dozen blows one of the staves splintered and brandy poured out onto the sand. I examined the keg again and saw that a second compartment had been built into the bottom third of it, and that it was almost intact. I smashed that open, and felt inside, and a moment later I drew out a package. It was a carefully sealed package, in a waterproof wrapping, and when I pressed it between my fingers the contents felt like powder.

I looked at Sutton. His face was ghastly in the lamplight. "What is it?" I said. "Dope?"

He gave a sulky nod. All the fight seemed to have gone out of him.

"I suppose when you came here alone on Thursday you were planning to clear off with it?"

"Naturally."

"How would you have known which keg to go for?"

"It was at the end of the row. I saw to that when we buried the stuff. There was a special mark on it."

"What about the rest of the kegs? We'd obviously have found them."

"It wouldn't have mattered—no one could prove who put them there. Ronnie was dead, and Jim would have kept his mouth shut for his own sake. I was going to rebury the broken keg somewhere else, that was all. I'd got everything worked out. If that damned stile hadn't collapsed when I was making sure you were asleep, I'd have got away with it."

George said: "Why didn't you come down and take the package away during the winter? You had plenty of time."

"I thought of it," said Sutton, "but it wouldn't have been easy." He had become surprisingly amenable again, and ready to talk. "If I'd started poking about here on my own Jim would have got suspicious, and there was the problem of getting tools to the spot, and the risk of bad weather. The stuff was safe enough where it was, and I decided it was better to be patient. We all make mistakes."

"I take it Ronnie wasn't in on this dope business?" I said.

"That noisy windbag! No, he was a child in these things. He thought it was just brandy."

I nodded. "Well, that seems to take care of everything. Except, of course, how we're going to get you back to St. Mary's."

Sutton got stiffly to his feet. "You needn't worry about that," he said. "I know when I'm licked. I'll come quietly."

At his mild tone we all relaxed a little. Then everything seemed to happen at once. He suddenly dived at me and snatched the package of dope and a second later he'd kicked out the hurricane lamp. For a few moments there was utter chaos. I heard a blow and a shout as Jim went flying backward into the trench, and then someone struck at me in the darkness and I grappled with a grunting body, only to discover it was George I was wrestling with. By the time we'd sorted ourselves out, Sutton was off along the cliff path with a twenty-yard start.

I suppose he had some wild notion of getting to the boats and marooning us on Samson while he rowed to St. Mary's and made his getaway—but this time he hadn't a hope. Jim caught and overpowered him as he was struggling with the painter of the white punt and we hauled him back ignominiously to the dig.

"Now what do we do with him?" said George, eying him as though he were some dangerous animal.

It was quite a problem. The idea of trying to row him to Hugh Town in the dark had become less attractive than ever.

"I suggest we light a fire," I said, "and sit it out till morning."

Jim nodded. He had settled himself on a keg beside the recumbent Sutton and was thumbing the edge of the axe.

"In that case," said George, as I began to look around for driftwood, "I think I'll go and get some biscuits."

20

Well, that's practically the end of the story. We got
Sutton safely to St. Mary's in one of the launches next day
and handed him over to the astonished constables. George
and Jim and I had a long session with the customs people
and in the evening two detectives came flying in from the
mainland and we had to go over everything again. Finally,
back came the reporters. Altogether, it was quite a day.

Jim, of course, had to face the music—not least from
Barney. I was very sorry for him, because a loathsome
racket like drug smuggling was about the last thing he'd
ever willingly have been involved in and he felt his position keenly. But the police seemed prepared to take a
lenient view of his part in the affair after an initial show

of severity and I gathered it was unlikely anything serious would happen to him. Long before my next visit to Scilly, I felt sure, he would have regained his natural buoyancy.

Sutton turned out to have a police record already. He was a clever, outwardly prepossessing blackguard, and some of the things that were read out about him in court just before he was sentenced were extraordinarily unsavory. Of course, he was only a part of a much larger organization, and the wider inquiries that followed his arrest were not entirely barren. But that's no part of this story.

Now that the Samson mystery was finally cleared up, I began to think about Olivia again. George was still urging me to go and see her—he seemed to imagine that because we'd at last proved something against Ronnie my path would be smoother! I couldn't share that view at all, but I knew now that I'd have to see her sooner or later and there was no point in waiting. Directly the police had finished with me I caught the express from Penzance, and the same evening I was ringing her up. It was about seven o'clock, and by good fortune she was at home. She said "Hullo!" rather coolly when I told her who it was, but she didn't say I mustn't call.

I took a taxi to her flat and she let me in herself. She was wearing a black dress and looked frightfully smart and self-assured against the lush background of her drawing room. I was terrified, and wondered if George would have been so confident about the outcome if he could have seen me at that moment.

She poured me a drink and I said I supposed she'd read about the smuggling business and she said she had and I said I was sorry about it all and she said she was sorry too and that she really didn't want to talk about it. After that there was an awkward pause. I stood looking at her, feeling an intrusive gawk and wondering how on earth I should begin to say what I'd come to say.

"Well?" she said unhelpfully.

I thought of all the things I'd rehearsed on the way up —how I would go back to the beginning of everything and explain step by step just how I'd come to act as I had and how natural it had been for me to get the wrong idea about her and how sorry I was and so on. But it all seemed so complicated and arid now, and in the end I just blurted out what was most in my mind.

"Olivia, I've been an utter fool and if you decide you never want to see me again I shan't be surprised. But I swear I never really believed in my heart what I said. I never wanted to believe it, not for a moment. I was trying all the time to prove to myself that you *hadn't* done it, because I was so desperately in love with you and I just couldn't bear it. . . ." I broke off. "Does that make any sense?"

She studied the golden liquid in her glass. "At least it's the nicest thing I've heard from you for some time."

"I could move on from that point," I said, "if you thought it would be any use." A faint smile lurked in her eyes and I felt encouraged. "I quite expect to have to work my passage home."

"And how would you propose to do that?"

"Well, I could stick around in London and perhaps we could get to know each other. Olivia, I love you so much I'm sure there must be a way . . ."

She turned aside so that I couldn't see her face. After a moment she said, "Personally, I blame George."

"Darling!" I had to laugh. "That's a little hard on him. I didn't have to listen to him, after all."

"And he didn't have to be so inhumanly logical and

212

clever. The trouble with George is that his mind's too active. He needs more exercise—let's send him a telegram."

She picked up the telephone receiver and asked for "Telegrams" and then she began to dictate. The wire she sent was: OLIVIA AND I DETAINED IN LONDON STOP PLEASE FILL IN TRENCH JOHN.

Then she hung up and gave me a smile and said, "Would you like to take me out to dinner?"